DEADLY ENCOUNTER

A commotion erupted, and Nate heard much thrashing and flailing. The scuffle was punctuated by the low growl of a beast and the strangled cry of a man. Suddenly, quiet descended once more.

What the blazes was going on out there? Nate wondered as he skirted the end of the thicket, trying to outflank the Indians on the right. His elbow struck a thin dead branch lying on the ground and it broke with a sharp crack.

Fuming at his stupidity, Nate rose into a crouch and dashed to the right. The Indians were bound to have heard and would easily pinpoint his position. He must put distance behind him or find a hiding place.

One moment he was adroitly weaving among the trees; the next someone hurtled out of the night and slammed into him from the rear. He was knocked forward, onto his knees, and when he frantically twisted to see his attacker he saw a tall warrior armed with a knife — a knife that streaked at his face.

The *Wilderness* series published by *Leisure Books:*

9

WILDERNESS

Mountain Devil

David Thompson

LEISURE BOOKS   NEW YORK CITY

Dedicated to Judy, Joshua, and Shane.
The best family a man could ever have.

A LEISURE BOOK®

March 1992

Published by

Dorchester Publishing Co., Inc.
276 Fifth Avenue
New York, NY 10001

Printed in the United States of America.

AUTHOR'S NOTE

Because it matters, the following story is based on fact.

During those years everything west of the Mississippi River was considered the exclusive domain of fierce beasts and savage Indians, a number of mountain men and bold explorers who traveled through what is now the northern United States and Canada took the time to record their experiences. These detailed narratives provide a wealth of information about the country, the people, and particularly the creatures they encountered. Some of those creatures defy identification. One such tale was reported by no less a personage than Theodore Roosevelt in his book *Wilderness Hunter,* published in 1892.

We still don't have the answer.

Chapter One

Someone—or *something*—was watching him.

Or so Nathaniel King believed, and he turned from the fine black stallion he had been rubbing down with a handful of soft green grass to survey the rugged countryside surrounding his remote cabin in the central Rockies. He was a big, broad-shouldered man with penetrating green eyes and a mane of black hair, and his brow furrowed as he searched for any sign of life, for any movement at all.

To the southeast a bald eagle soared, hunting prey. To the north an irate squirrel chattered. East of the cabin lay a lake teeming with ducks and other fowl, and on its southern shore stood four black-tailed deer, a buck and three doe.

Nate saw nothing to arouse alarm and allowed himself to relax. He resumed stroking the stallion, the buckskins that covered his supple frame flowing with the motions of his muscular arms and shoulders. Angled across his powerful chest was a powder horn and a bullet pouch. In a beaded sheath on his left hip hung a butcher knife, while tucked under his wide brown leather belt were two flintlock pistols, one on either side of the buckle. An eagle feather had been tied at the back of his hair with the quill jutting upwards.

As Nate worked, the nagging feeling persisted that he was being observed. He repeatedly glanced over his shoulders, wondering each time if his nerves were getting the better of him. Not that he didn't have cause for being concerned. Living close to Ute country as he did, he never knew when the resentful Utes might decide to pay him a visit and try to wipe out his entire family. The Utes despised whites, and they went out of their way to exterminate any mountaineers they found.

Nate finished rubbing down the stallion and tossed the grass aside, then turned to exit the stout corral attached to the south side of his cabin. Nearby, milling about, were the five other horses he owned. He paused at the rails to retrieve his prized Hawken rifle, then climbed out. A cool breeze from the northwest stirred his hair. Inhaling deeply, he smelled the tangy scent of pine and the dank odor of the rich earth that carpeted the lush valley he'd staked out as his own.

The cabin door opened and out came his lovely wife, Winona. A full-blooded Shoshone, she had long dark hair and matching eyes. A buckskin dress clung to her shapely figure, and cradled in the crook of her left arm was a basket.

"Where are you going?" Nate inquired in English.

"To gather eggs for our supper," Winona answered, closing the door behind her. She smiled and headed for the lake.

The thought of a savory omelet made Nate's mouth water. He gazed at the sunny sky, grateful winter had ended. The early April weather had been exceptionally mild, and soon he must leave to get some trapping done if he hoped to take a large number of prime beaver pelts to the annual rendezvous held in the summer. "Is Zachary sleeping?" he thought to ask before Winona went too far.

She halted and pivoted. "I thought he was with you."

"What?" Nate said, stiffening.

"He went out to help you with the horses a while ago," Winona explained, retracing her steps, her tone betraying a hint of anxiety.

Nate looked every which way. "He never came near the corral," he said, keeping his voice calm, telling himself there was no need to become apprehensive . . . yet. Their three-year-old son was notorious for wandering off without a word to either one of them. Unfortunately, what with the many predators in the area, not to mention the ever-present prospect of the Utes showing up, wandering off could prove fatal.

"Not again," Winona said.

"You go north, I'll go south," Nate proposed. "Keep yelling until he replies."

"I hope he doesn't hide from us."

"He'd better not. I warned him what would happen if he did that one more time."

They separated, Nate skirting the corral and entering the dense trees. "Zachary!" he bellowed, startling sparrows in a thicket. "Where are you?"

From north of the cabin came Winona's voice. "Zachary! Zachary!"

For several minutes Nate hiked and shouted. The boy didn't respond. Worry battled with anger for supremacy in Nate's mind. There were times, he mused, when being a parent tried his patience to its limits. On several occasions he'd been strongly tempted to apply his belt to his son's backside, and only the promise he'd made to Winona shortly after Zach was born had stopped him. They'd agreed to raise the boy in the Shoshone fashion, which meant never striking him no matter how badly he misbehaved. Instead, they tried to influence Zachary's behavior by always exhorting him to do what was proper and good and by setting ideal examples themselves. Talk about difficult tasks. Nate often marveled that Indians resorted to such exacting child-rearing practices when a good spanking would be so much easier to apply and would bear more immediate fruit. How well he recollected the many spankings his father had given him, and he'd turned out okay.

He wondered if Zachary was playing at being an Indian warrior again. Sometimes the boy would pretend to be a mighty brave on a raid, and during this play Zach would only answer to his Shoshone name. "Stalking Coyote!" he called out. "Time to come back to your village."

The forest mocked him with its silence. All his shouting had caused every living creature within hearing distance to become quiet.

"Young man, this is your father!" Nate yelled angrily. "If you're listening, I demand you answer me this instant."

A bee buzzed past him.

Nate halted at the base of a knoll, the Hawken in his left hand. Far off Winona still shouted. He couldn't imagine the boy straying so far, but he decided to climb to the top of the knoll for a look-see before returning to the cabin. Hastening upward, he stopped on the crest and made a complete revolution, idly noting the towering ring of snow-capped peaks rimming the valley even as he probed the underbrush. Not so much as a rabbit stirred. Convinced he was wasting his time, he turned to depart, and his gaze landed on a boulder-strewn hill approximately a hundred yards to the southwest.

A diminutive figure marched resolutely toward the top.

"Zachary!" Nate thundered, and ran in pursuit. Promise or no promise, the boy's breach of discipline deserved harsh punishment. Time and time again, Winona and he had warned Zachary about going more than a few feet from the cabin when unescorted. The boy simply couldn't get it into his inexperienced head that there were great dangers lurking in the woods. Just once Nate would like to see Zachary have a serious scare that would bring the boy to his senses. Just once—

Something else moved on that hill, something big and long and tawny, something creeping down the slope toward the unsuspecting child.

It was a panther.

Some trappers called them mountain lions. Some referred to them as cougars. Nate used the term favored by the majority of trappers. However they were known, the big cats were renowned for their stealth and their ferocity when aroused. And the sight of one stalking his son sparked a ripple of stark fear down Nate's spine.

"Zachary!" Nate bellowed, and raced toward the hill. His son stopped, turned, and waved. "Come down!" he yelled, motioning with his free arm for the boy to descend, but Zachary resumed climbing.

The panther, 20 yards above the child, paused and glanced at Nate. Then it effortlessly vaulted onto the top of a large, flat boulder and crouched at the lip where it could see the slope below and mark the progress of its intended victim.

Such a bold cat was exceedingly rare. Usually mountain lions fled at the sight or scent of humans. This one, Nate speculated, must be famished, or else believed Zachary to be such easy prey that it wasn't about to stop stalking him just because another person had shown up. He saw Zachary wend among some boulders and opened his mouth to scream. "Zach! Come back! There's a panther above you."

The boy kept going.

Nate knew he wouldn't reach the hill in time to prevent the cat from reaching his son. He must act, and act now, if he hoped to have Zachary grow to a ripe old age. Accordingly, he abruptly halted, snapped the Hawken to his right shoulder, and cocked it. He sighted along the barrel, fixing the bead on the panther's head. It would be a long shot and he couldn't be certain of scoring, but it was his only hope. To compensate for the distance he elevated the barrel to where he instinctively felt it should be, then held his breath and steadied the rifle.

Crouching low, the panther fixed its hungry gaze on Zachary and coiled to spring.

Please let me hit it! Nate prayed, and squeezed the trigger. The Hawken blasted, belching smoke and lead, and on the flat boulder the cougar suddenly recoiled and twisted sharply to one side as the ball nicked its left shoulder, causing blood and flesh to spray outward. Snarling, the cat stared balefully at Nate.

Appalled that the shot hadn't killed it, Nate sped onward. He wouldn't waste time reloading the rifle. If he could get close enough, he'd employ both flintlock pistols.

Little Zachary had halted at the loud retort and now stood watching his father approach. Beaming, he waved happily.

"Come here!" Nate cried on the run. "Come here this instant!"

Finally the boy obeyed. His slender shoulders slumping in resignation, he headed down the hill.

Nate's eyes were locked on the big cat. The panther glanced at Zach, then vented a loud, angry growl. It took a tentative step, as if about to leap from the boulder and attack, but its head turned toward Nate once more and, with remarkable alacrity, it whirled and went up the hill covering 15 feet in a bound. In moments it was gone over the crest, back into the heart of wilderness from which it had emerged.

"Zachary!" Nate cried in relief. The boy stopped at the base of the hill and waited for him, and when he got there he sank to his knees and impulsively gave his son a firm hug. He closed his eyes and held Zachary for almost a minute, overwhelmed with gratitude for the child's deliverance.

"Pa?"

Nate drew back and coughed to clear a constriction in his throat. "Didn't you see the panther?" he asked gruffly.

"Where?" Zachary responded excitedly, and looked all around for the beast. "Show me."

"It ran off," Nate said. "But if I hadn't shown up when I did, it would have eaten you."

Zachary giggled at the prospect. "Panther not eat me. Me hit it," he declared, and swung his tiny right fist at an imaginary cougar.

Under different circumstances Nate would have laughed at the comically determined expression his son wore. But this was serious. The boy had nearly been slain. He maintained a stern face and said, "You can't stop a panther with your bare hands."

"Me could. Me strong."

"You're not strong enough," Nate said harshly. "Anyway, the panther is not the main issue here. Going off by yourself is. Why did you wander away from the cabin when you've been told time and again not to do so?"

"Me saw a butterfly."

"A butterfly?"

Zachary nodded and used his right hand to mimic

the flapping motion of a butterfly's wing. "Yes. It flied past the cabin and me try to catch it."

"Oh," Nate said, and sighed. The boy had been intensely interested in bugs for the last six months or so. Every bug Zach saw, he had to catch and examine. Nate could well imagine how hard it would be for Zach to resist the fluttering temptation of a colorful butterfly, but he still couldn't let the violation go unpunished. "So you ran after it and didn't bother to tell your mother or me."

Zachary, in his youthful innocence, answered promptly and honestly. It never occurred to him to lie. "Yes, me did."

"Say '*I* did,'" Nate corrected him.

"You did?"

"No, you did."

"But you said—"

"Never mind," Nate declared, and took the boy into his right arm. Rising, the Hawken in his left hand, he pivoted and headed for the cabin. "You can't keep doing this, son. One of these days we won't realize you've gone off and a panther or a grizzly or something else will get you."

"Me not scared," Zachary stated.

"I know. And that's part of the problem. You'd be better off if you *were* scared."

"Me *should* be scared?" Zachary asked in amazement.

Nate nodded. "A man who claims he's never been scared is either a liar or a fool. Fear can be good for you if you don't give in to it. It teaches you to be cautious, to play it safe instead of being reckless and getting yourself killed. Do you understand?"

Zachary shook his head. "Me never scared. Me just like you."

"I've been scared plenty of times."

"You have?"

"More times than I care to remember," Nate admitted. "And I'm here today because I learned how to cope with my fear and do what had to be done anyway."

"Tell me some of the times," Zachary requested.

So Nate did, detailing his several terrifying encounters with grizzly bears and his battles with hostile Indians. He told about the time a rattler nearly bit him, and the time he was attacked by a savage wolverine. His son listened intently, eyes agleam with the thrill of adventure. Nate concluded his narrative as they came up on the rear of the cabin. "So you can see that I've been scared many times and it's nothing to be ashamed of. Just don't let your fear stop you from doing whatever has to be done."

"Me won't, Pa. Me chase butterflies anyway."

"That isn't what I meant," Nate muttered, angling around the south end of the corral while racking his brain for a way of getting through to his son, of making his meaning clear. Engrossed in his thoughts, he didn't realize they weren't alone until he stepped in front of the pen and glanced up to discover three mounted men near the front door.

Chapter Two

"Look Pa!" Zachary cried in delight. "Peoples!"

The boy was excited because visitors to their remote cabin were few and far between. Nate didn't share his son's enthusiasm. From bitter prior experience he knew that sometimes visitors spelled trouble, deadly trouble, and the moment he laid eyes on the trio he gently deposited Zachary at his feet and straightened, deliberately hooking the thumb on his right hand in his leather belt close to the right flintlock. He'd foolishly neglected to reload the Hawken after shooting at the panther, but he had two good pistols and a butcher knife he could employ to decidedly lethal effect should these strangers prove to be unfriendly. "Howdy," he said, keeping his tone reserved, his features impassive.

Zachary started to move toward the men.

"Stand still," Nate ordered severely, and the boy stopped and glanced up at him in startled surprise.

The three men were all armed, but they made no

move to bring their weapons into play. All three wore buckskins, the typical attire of mountaineers and Indians alike. Two of the trio were whites; the third was an old Crow warrior whose hair was almost white from age and whose face resembled a craggy bluff. The nearest white sat astride a black gelding and wore a blue cloth cap of the type initially popular with Canadian *voyageurs*, Canadian trappers, and now worn by many of their counterparts in the lower Rockies. He was tall and lean and sported a full black beard. The other white man was on a bay. He was stocky and clean-shaven and wore a string of bear teeth around his neck. Both whites were showing teeth.

"Howdy, friend," the tall one said. "My name is Milo Benteen." He nodded at the stocky man. "This is Tom Sublette. We're both from Pennsylvania and we came out here to do some trapping a year ago."

Nate simply bobbed his chin. He was thinking about Winona, wondering what had happened to her, and no sooner did the thought cross his mind than she emerged from the cabin casually holding a rifle in the crook of her left arm. She looked at him and smiled, then stood still and faced the men.

All three newcomers glanced at her, at the rifle, then at Nate.

"Are you folks expecting trouble?" Milo asked.

"You never know," Nate responded.

Milo cast a shocked expression at Tom, then turned to Nate and said, "Are you referring to us? Hell, man, we don't mean you any harm. We came all this way searching for you to offer you a proposition."

"Oh?" Nate said, not yet ready to accept them as friendly. Some years back he'd taken a stranger into his home, fed and sheltered the man, and when the stranger's companions later arrived they had abducted Winona and left him for dead. He wasn't ever going to make that mistake again.

"That is, if you're Nathaniel King," Tom Sublette threw in.

"I am."

Milo beamed. "At last. Do you have any idea how hard it was for us to track you down? We heard about you at the rendezvous last year. They say you're one of the best, as good as Jim Bridger or Shakespeare McNair. They say you brought in over six hundred pelts one year."

"Six hundred and forty-two," Nate said.

"They also say you're honest to a fault and as dependable as they come," Tom mentioned. "We were told we could trust you with our lives."

"How did you find my cabin?" Nate inquired. So far as he knew, only his good friend Shakespeare McNair and two other trappers knew its exact location. It wasn't wise to advertise where one lived; enemies might find out and pay you a visit.

"Once we decided it was you we wanted, we asked around," Milo said. "Ran into a man named Cumberland who is a close friend of McNair's. Cumberland told us he believed you lived in this general area but he couldn't pinpoint where. So for the past two weeks we've been traipsing all over this stretch of mountains looking for you."

"Why?" Nate asked.

Milo shifted in his saddle. "We've been riding for hours. Do you reckon we could light and sit a spell?"

Nate hesitated, thinking of the consequences for Winona and Zach if he made the wrong decision. But these men seemed sincere. All three had rifles, but they had studiously refrained from so much as touching the long guns resting across their thighs. If they'd meant to harm him and his family, they could easily have lain in ambush and gunned him down when his back was turned. He suddenly recalled the feeling he'd had earlier of being watched and gazed up at Benteen. "Were you watching us earlier?"

Milo blinked. "We first saw your cabin from across the lake yonder. I took out my telescope for a look-see. Cumberland gave us a description of you and I wanted to see if we'd lucked out and found you. How did you know?"

"I knew," Nate said, and let it go at that. He took Zach's small hand in his and walked to the door. "Why don't you climb down and tie your animals at the corral? My wife will fix us a pot of coffee and you can explain the reason you've sought me out."

"Thanks," Milo said.

Winona took Zachary inside while Nate watched the three men move to the corral and dismount. The old Crow had not said a word. Nate studied the warrior's face, trying to determine the man's character in the many lines and creases. For such an oldster, the Crow held himself erect and displayed remarkable vitality. Nate knew quite a few elderly Indians who could hold their own with 20-year-olds, and suspected their outstanding longevity and physical prowess was attributable to the Indian way of life, to drinking only pure water and eating the freshest of foods and breathing the clear mountain air. He remembered how it was back in New York City and other cities and towns, where the smoke from burning coal and wood in the winter would form heavy clouds that made a person cough and stung the eyes, and how food served at home or at eating establishments would be steeped in salt and invariably overcooked. It was a wonder white men lived to be 60, let alone 80 and older as did many Indians.

He waited and allowed them to go in first, then followed and leaned the Hawken against the wall to the left of the doorway. The cabin was comfortably furnished. A large table near the center of the spacious single room was ringed by four wooden chairs. Off to one side against the wall sat the bed. A stone fireplace was directly opposite the door and a new bearskin rug lay in front of the hearth. Beaded leather curtains covered the one window, compliments of Winona. Her feminine touches were everywhere, from the flowers in a clay vase to the decorated parfleches hanging on one wall. It was her handiwork, Nate reflected, that had transformed the cabin into a home.

"Nice place you have here, Mr. King," Milo Benteen commented.

"Call me Nate. Why don't you gents take a seat?"

All three sat down, leaving empty the chair facing the entrance. Nate walked over, turned it around, and straddled it so he could rest his forearms on top of the crest, leaving his hands free to draw the pistols if need be. He still wasn't taking any chances.

"We're glad we found you at home," Tom said. "We were afraid you'd be out doing your spring trapping."

"A few more days and I would have been," Nate said, glancing to his left where Zachary was playing with a toy rifle he'd whittled from a tree limb. Winona was busy preparing the coffee.

"We'll get straight to the point," Milo Benteen stated, leaning forward on his elbows. "Tom and I came out here with the hope of catching enough beaver to provide both of us with the stakes we'd need to buy homesteads for the families we hope to have one day. We know that an average trapper makes about two thousand dollars selling his hides at the annual rendezvous, which is quite a bit of money considering a mason or a carpenter only makes about six hundred a year."

Nate listened patiently, well aware of the economic facts of life for trappers and laborers alike.

"But we'll be honest with you," Milo went on,

"We've tried trapping for a year and had a darned hard time of it. Between the two of us we've only made three hundred dollars so far."

"Trapping can be rough," Nate said to hold up his end of the conversation.

"And we've heard that it's getting harder every year," Tom interjected. "The old-timers tells us there aren't as many beaver around as there used to be. The best streams, those easiest to get to, have all been pretty much trapped out. To find prime pelts nowadays a person has to go deep into the remote valleys."

"I know," Nate agreed. He never would have believed it was possible, but beaver were becoming harder to find with each passing year. When he'd first ventured to the Rockies, there had been so many beaver that he'd scoffed at the idea the critters would ever be trapped out.

"We became discouraged," Milo confessed, "and we were considering heading back to Pennsylvania when we bumped into Red Moon here." He indicated the Crow with a jerk of his thumb. "He told us about a valley where the beaver are as thick as flies on a rotting buffalo carcass, where three or four men could go in, spend three or four months trapping, and come out with five hundred pelts or more *apiece*."

Nate looked at the old warrior, trying not to let his skepticism show. He'd been all over the region and he knew of no such valley. He wondered if Red Moon was a drinker. Some of the Indians became addicted to alcohol and were prone to telling tall tales when they were under the influence. For that matter, many of the whites were the same way.

"Tom and I want to trap this valley," Milo said, excitement in his tone. "Red Moon has agreed to take us there in exchange for ten percent of our profits."

Nate performed some hasty mental calculations. If the beaver were as thick as the Crow claimed, and if

Tom and Milo each made about two thousand dollars, that would give the Crow four hundred in pocket money, which was more than most Indians saw in a lifetime. He wondered what the warrior wanted with so much currency. Generally speaking, Indians had little use for the white's man scrip.

"But Tom and I know our limitations," Milo stated. "We're pretty green. We figure we need someone else to throw in with us, someone who has trapped for years and knows the profession inside out, someone who has a reputation as being one of the best in the business." He paused and bored his eyes into Nate. "Someone like you."

So this was the reason for their visit. Nate saw all three men gaze expectantly at him and leaned back, stretching, buying time to think. He preferred to trap alone. Most trappers did, simply because each had favorite areas and didn't want anyone else moving in and taking pelts away from them. Then too, most trappers were loners, highly independent men who could go for months without seeing another living soul and not be bothered by it in the least.

"Would you be interested?" Milo asked hopefully.

Nate had to admit to himself the proposal was intriguing. If the valley was rich in beaver, if no one had ever laid a trap line there before, then every one of them stood to earn top dollar for their peltries. He might make more money than he would trapping alone. "I'm interested," he said, "but I have reservations."

"What are they?" Tom Sublette inquired.

Twisting, Nate stared at the Crow. Since the warrior had told Benteen and Sublette about the valley and neither of them had been in the mountains long enough to learn much of the Crow tongue and likely weren't greatly proficient at sign language, he figured the oldster must know English. "I've lived in these mountains for some time," he noted. "Why haven't I heard of this valley before?"

Red Moon answered in a soft voice, his English clipped and precise. "No whites have ever been there."

"What about your people?"

"My people have not gone there in many, many winters."

The disclosure struck Nate as peculiar. "Is it located in Crow country?" he asked.

"Yes. Far to the north."

"Which means it's close to Blackfeet country," Nate said.

Benteen glanced from the Crow to Nate. "Is that important?"

"Haven't you heard about the Blackfeet? They're the scourge of the Rockies. They despise whites and kill every one they find. More trappers have lost their lives to those devils than to any other tribe. I've tangled with them a few times and I'm lucky to still be wearing my hair."

"I'm willing to take the risk," Tom Sublette said.

"Have you ever fought the Blackfeet?" Nate asked.

"No," Tom answered.

"Then don't be so eager to lose your scalp," Nate cautioned, and turned to the Crow again. "Tell me, Red Moon. Do the Crows stay away from this valley because they don't want to run into the Blackfeet?"

"No."

"When was the last time the Crows were there?"

"Twelve winters ago one of our bravest warriors, Crooked Nose, went there. He never returned."

"The Blackfeet must have got ahold of him," Milo Benteen commented.

"No," Red Moon said.

Nate lightly drummed his fingers on the table, pondering. He was convinced the brave had not revealed everything he knew about the valley, perhaps deliberately. But what? And why? "You sound as if you know what happened to Crooked Nose. Do you?"

"Yes. He was killed."

"If the Blackfeet weren't responsible, who was?"

"Not who. What."

"An animal killed him?" Nate asked. Even Indians, with their wealth of woodlore and their ability to move silently and unseen through the forest, occasionally fell prey to grizzlies or panthers or other predators.

"No," Red Moon said, and sighed. "Crooked Nose was slain by the thing that lurks in the dark."

Chapter Three

For a full five seconds no one said a word. Milo Ben-teen and Tom Sublette wore amused expressions, as if they thought the statement had been some sort of joke.

Nate knew better. He'd lived among Indians long enough to be able to pick up subtle nuances of behavior and intent other whites often missed. Red Moon had been deathly serious; his eyes had registered the faintest hint of deeply buried apprehension when mentioning the "thing" that had slain Crooked Nose.

"What is this?" Milo broke the silence. "What kind of critter are you talking about?"

"I do not know," Red Moon said softly.

"But you Indians know everything there is to know about the animals in these mountains," Tom noted. "Was it a bear or a big cat or what?"

"It was none of those," Red Moon said, staring at

each of them in turn. "It was ..." and then he used a Crow word with which Nate was unfamiliar.

"Say it in English," Milo said.

"There is no English word for the thing that lives in the valley," Red Moon replied. "So I just call it the *thing*."

"You're not making any sense," Tom stated. "What's this thing look like?"

"I do not know. No one has ever seen it and lived to tell what he saw."

Milo laughed. "Oh, come now, Red Moon. Is this another of your silly Indian superstitions like all those demons and other spirit creatures your people believe in?"

"The thing in the valley is not a spirit. It is flesh and bone, like you and I. It can touch and be touched. It can kill and has done so many times."

Insight flared in Nate and he cleared his throat. "Your people stopped going into the valley because of this creature?" he inquired.

"Yes," Red Moon confirmed. "Even though the valley has much game, with deer and elk and beaver everywhere, we no longer go there to hunt. Crooked Nose was the last to do so, and he suffered the same fate as have a dozen warriors over the years."

"How many years are you talking about?" Milo asked.

"The creature has lived there for over seventy winters, so far as we know. Perhaps it has been there much longer. Perhaps it has lived there since the beginning of all things."

Both Milo and Tom laughed.

"Have you ever heard such nonsense?" Tom said, addressing no one in particular. "It must be an old grizzly, and the four of us can handle any bear that rears its ugly head."

"Why didn't you mention this critter sooner?" Milo asked the Crow.

"I did not want you to change your minds about going," Red Moon answered.

Tom chuckled. "You were afraid this spook tale of yours would scare us off? Red Moon, you don't know us very well. Milo and I aren't scared of anything, and that especially goes for Injun hokum." He paused. "No offense meant."

Nate was speculating on the implications of the warrior's comments. Why, if Red Moon firmly believed this mysterious creature existed, was the Crow willing to brave its wrath by venturing into a valley that was shunned by the entire tribe? Did Red Moon need the money so badly he was willing to risk his life to get it? And if so, what did he want with the money anyway? Indians invariably traded for whatever they wanted. They had no need for money.

"Hold on a second," Milo said. "I've been doing some figuring. You say Crooked Nose was killed how many winters ago?"

"Twelve."

"Hell, man. That's twelve years. For all you know, the grizzly or whatever killed him is long dead by now."

"The thing that lurks in the dark will never die," Red Moon said.

Milo looked at Nate. "Have you ever heard tell of critters like the one he claims is in this valley?"

"No."

"I have."

The declaration came from Winona. She was standing to one side, holding two tin cups in each hand. Now she placed them on the table and gazed meaningfully at her husband. "My people have known of such creatures too. We call them the Giants of the Night. They lived in this land before my people came, and our legends tell of how our brave warriors drove most of the Giants away after great battles." She paused and glanced at the Crow. "I did not know there were any still around."

"Giants?" Tom Sublette repeated, and snickered. "Ma'am, there have been mountaineers in these parts ever since Lewis and Clark set foot out here. That's well-nigh thirty years. You'd think that if there were strange critters running around, most of the trappers and such would know about it by now."

"I know what I know," Winona said, and went to the hearth to retrieve the coffeepot.

Milo turned to Nate. "I hope you won't let this foolishness get to you. It must be a bear, nothing more. We were told that your Indian name is Grizzly Killer, that you've killed more grizzlies than any other trapper alive, so the idea of facing another shouldn't worry you none."

"Facing any grizzly worries me. They're not to be taken lightly," Nate said, thinking back to that distant day when he'd killed his first silver-tip while crossing the plains with his Uncle Zeke. Since then he had been through several horrifying encounters with the fearsome giant bears and nearly perished on each occasion. If there was an old grizzly living in the valley, he didn't relish confronting it. Nor did he view the bear as reason enough to put off trapping there when they each stood to make a couple of thousand dollars from the enterprise. They would have to remain alert, and if the bear showed, kill it. It was as simple as that.

"Will you throw in with us?" Tom asked bluntly.

"Your offer is intriguing," Nate told them. "I'm definitely interested, but I need some time to think about it and discuss it with my wife." He gazed at the window. "How soon were you fixing to head on out?"

"Any time you're ready," Milo responded. "Our pack animals are down by the lake in a clearing. They were plumb tuckered out after the long climb up to this hideaway of yours so we left them there to rest and came on ahead."

"How about if you let us know in the morning?" Tom proposed. "Would that give you enough time to make up your mind?"

"More than enough," Nate said. "I'll give you my decision at dawn, then."

Winona brought over the coffeepot and poured each of them a full cup of the steaming brew. Over an hour was spent in idle conversation, with Nate eliciting information from the two Pennsylvanians about the latest news in the States and sharing information about his years in the Rockies and the trapping business in general.

He learned that a new religious group calling themselves the Mormons had sprung up and were causing quite a stir. They had been driven out of New York after being relentlessly persecuted by those who regarded them as blasphemous. He heard that a slave named Nat Turner had instigated a revolt in Virginia. The insurrection was speedily crushed and many innocent blacks slain by the outraged whites. And he also listened to a fascinating story about a new hotel in Boston that was the talk of the East. Apparently this hotel had installed elegant imported indoor water closets that were all the rage. Folks would travel hundreds of miles and take a room just to be able to use the newfangled bathroom facilities.

"And did you hear about the *Fulton I*?" Milo asked.

"No. What about it?" Nate replied. The *Fulton I* had been designed and constructed by the famous inventor Robert Fulton. It was Fulton who had built the first commercially successful steamboat, the *Clermont*, back in 1801. The *Fulton I*, authorized by Congress in 1814, was the world's first steam-powered warship and had been put into service specifically for the defense of New York Harbor.

"It went and blew up," Milo related. "Caused by some kind of breakdown in the engine, I think the newspapers said."

Tom Sublette took a sip of coffee. "And I guess you've heard about the trouble brewing down Texas way?"

"No, I haven't," Nate admitted. Texas was a province of Mexico, and all he knew about it was that it was terribly hot in the summer and took a man forever to cross on horseback. Or so many of the tall-tale tellers claimed.

"There might be a shooting war down thataway in the next couple of years," Tom mentioned. "A lot of Americans have drifted to Texas to live, and by all accounts they're none too happy with the way Mexico is running the province. Our government is interested in buying Texas like we did all that land in the Louisiana Purchase, but when an envoy was sent down to Mexico City to make the Mexican government an offer, they sent him back with his tail between his legs."

"A lot of folks back in the States are riled by the whole affair," Milo added. "The former governor of Tennessee, Sam Houston, has gone there to see about bringing independence to the province, and the Mexicans aren't likely to sit still for any meddling in their country."

"I wish those folks luck, whatever they decide to do," Nate commented, "but it doesn't concern me."

Then the two Pennsylvanians plied him with questions about the state of affairs among the various tribes. He knew little they didn't already know. How the Blackfeet, the Pagans, and the Bloods were still united in a confederacy that controlled all of the northern plains region and most of the northern Rockies. How the Kiowas were giving travelers on the

Santa Fe Trail a hard time. And how the Nez Percés and the Flatheads had sent delegations all the way to St. Louis to request religious instruction for their respective tribes.

At that remark Nate saw Milo Benteen glance thoughtfully at Winona, and he could deduce the man's thoughts. Benteen was wondering what it must be like to have an Indian woman for a wife, and how the differences in cultures were reconciled. To Benteen's credit, the man had been in the Rockies long enough to know not to pry into the personal affairs of other folks and he didn't voice any of the questions filtering through his mind.

"Well, I reckon we should go check on our horses," Milo said, rising. "Ma'am, the coffee was delicious."

"Thank you," Winona said.

Nate also stood. "You can keep your animals in our corral for the night, if you wish. They won't wander off and you won't need to fret about prowling panthers so much."

"We're grateful," Milo said. "We'll bed down under the trees and await your decision come morning."

"Fair enough," Nate responded. "And we'd be happy if you'd join us for supper. My wife can make the best venison stew this side of the continental divide."

Tom beamed and licked his lips. "Home cooking! Why, I haven't tasted a home-cooked meal in a coon's age. Be sure and have Winona make extra."

Nate laughed. "We'll fill the pot to the brim," he promised, and escorted them out to their mounts. The trappers waved, Red Moon nodded, and off they rode.

"They're nice men, Pa," Zachary said at Nate's side. "Me like them."

"Me too," Nate absently replied, and instantly regretted it.

"See? You say 'me,'" the boy pointed out.

"Yes, but it's not the same. You're supposed to say 'I' most of the time when you're talking about yourself."

"Then why is there a word called 'me'?"

"Because you use that at times too."

His smooth brow knit in confusion, Zachary shook his head and declared, "Me no understand when me is I and I is me."

"We'll sit down and go over your English after I get back," Nate said, turning toward the cabin. Winona stood in the doorway, and she gave him a troubled look, wheeled, then went in. He picked up Zach and carried the boy inside, setting him near the table. Winona was at the fireplace, adding a few small limbs to the flames. "I take it you don't think I should go?"

"I do not like the idea, husband, no."

"If what Red Moon says is true about all the beaver in this valley, I could collect three times the amount of pelts I ordinarily would in half the time. I can be home from trapping that much sooner."

"If you live," Winona said, her shoulders held stiffly.

"Do you believe his story about the thing that lurks in the dark?"

"I would not take it lightly."

Nate sat down and rested his feet on the edge of the table. "All right. Let's talk this out. Let's accept for the moment that there is some kind of strange critter up there, something few Indians have seen and fewer white men even know about." He paused to get her attention and she faced him. "Didn't you tell us that long ago your own people fought these Giants and drove them out of your country?"

"That is the legend the old men tell."

Nate shrugged. "Then I don't see where we have much to worry about. Your people used bows and lances back then. We'll have four rifles among us and pistols besides. Even if this critter is as hard to die as a grizzly, we can kill it."

"Didn't you say grizzlies should not be taken lightly?" Winona asked softly.

"Yes. And you know me well enough to know I'm not about to take any reckless chances. If we find any grizzly sign in this valley, I'll track it down and we'll dispatch it right off so we can run our trap lines in safety. And you know I'm a damn good tracker thanks to Shakespeare."

"You are one of the best trackers alive, Indian or white," Winona agreed.

Nate rose, walked up to her, and put his hands on her shoulders. The concern in her eyes touched him deeply. "Dearest, I'm only thinking of us. We could use a good haul of peltries. And I like the idea of getting my trapping down well before the end of the season. It means I'll have more time to spend with Zachary and you."

"So you have made up your mind?"

"Not yet, but I'll confess I'm leaning toward going," Nate said, and tenderly embraced her. He kissed her lightly on the lips and smiled, trying to cheer her up. "Don't worry. I'm not about to let some old legend stop me from coming back to you. And I'll swing by Shakespeare's cabin on the way out and ask him to check on Zach and you every now and then. Knowing him, he'll probably ride on over and move in until I return. So you have no need to get all bothered. Everything will be fine. You'll see."

Winona made no reply, but Nate swore he felt her tremble slightly in his arms.

Chapter Four

The four men rode out the next morning two hours after sunrise.

Nate had agonized all night over whether he should go. He tried to sleep but caught only snatches now and then. Beside him Winona slumbered fitfully, tossing and turning more than she normally did and mumbling words in the Shoshone tongue occasionally. The only word she said loud enough for him to understand was "beast."

The determining factor in his decision to go was his family. He simply couldn't afford to let such a golden opportunity pass. They could use the money. And, as he'd told her, he liked the idea of completing his trapping season early so they would have more time together.

Shortly before dawn he slipped out of bed, donned his buckskins, wedged his pistols under his belt, and went outside. Red Moon was already awake, seated quietly at the base of a tall tree and gazing thoughtfully at the gradually brightening eastern horizon. Nate informed the Crow he would go, and Red Moon said he would tell the two Pennsylvanians when they woke up.

Tiptoeing back inside, Nate found Winona sitting up. There was no need to tell her his decision. He knew that she knew from her troubled expression and the hint of anxiety in her lovely eyes. She didn't protest, though, or complain. She simply got up, got dressed, and began preparing breakfast. Then she helped him pack the supplies and trapping gear he must take along.

There was a lot of it. Not only must he take enough flour, jerky, coffee, and other foodstuffs to tide him over for an extended period, food he would naturally supplement by killing wild game as needed, but he must tote a dozen Newhouse traps, each of which weighed about six pounds, two skinning knives and fleshing tools, a heavy axe and a light tomahawk, extra fire steels and tinder boxes, blankets, assorted small tools, and odds and ends.

Most of the trapping gear was stored in the southwest corner of the cabin where it was handy for packing. Since they knew the routine by heart, they had the pair of packhorses Nate wanted to take fully loaded within an hour. Zachary helped, carrying small items when requested and repeatedly dashing outside to give Benteen and Sublette status reports on their progress.

The Pennsylvanians were mounted and patiently waiting when Nate loaded the last pack and went inside to get the Hawken. Winona stood to the left of the door, out of sight of the three men. Her eyes said everything.

Nate enfolded her in his arms, their cheeks touching, her warm breath on his ear. She hugged him tighter than she ordinarily did, much tighter, almost as if she expected it to be the last time she would do so, but her eyes were dry and her face proud when he stepped back and smiled. "Take care of yourself."

"I will."

"I'll miss you. You know that."

"And I you."

"I will carry you with me always, right here," Nate said, and tapped his chest above his heart. He kissed her then, a lingering kiss, savoring the feel of her lips and tongue. When he straightened, small arms looped around his left leg and he glanced down.

"Me miss you, Pa."

Nate lifted Zach and hugged him. "I'll think of you every minute I'm gone," he said. "You're the man of the house while I'm away, so you be good and help your mother. Listen to her at all times."

"Me will."

"And don't wander off like you did yesterday."

"Me won't."

Feeling a constriction in his throat, Nate kissed the boy, then laughed and said, "Me love you, little one."

The Pennsylvanians had their mounts turned to the northwest when he emerged and climbed onto his black stallion. "I'm ready, gents," he announced. "And if you don't mind, I'd like to stop by the cabin of a friend of mine and ask him to keep watch on my family during my absence. He's my nearest neighbor. Lives about twenty-five miles north of here."

"Fine by us," Milo said. "Who is he?"

"Shakespeare McNair."

"*The* Shakespeare McNair?" Tom blurted out.

"Yep," Nate said. He looked at his wife and son, standing rather forlornly side by side in the doorway, gave a little wave, and forced himself to face forward and ride off, the lead to the two pack animals in his left hand. Twenty yards from the cabin he twisted in

the saddle and looked over his shoulder. Winona and
Zach both waved and he did likewise. Leaving them
periodically to go off trapping taxed his self-control
to its limits. He hated leaving them alone. But he had
to make a living. He was a free trapper, and since the
beaver weren't about to march up to his front door
and lie down to be skinned, he must go where the
beaver were. Still, thinking of all the grizzlies and
panthers in the Rockies and the constant threat of the
Utes didn't make departing any easier.

"We've heard McNair is a good friend of yours,"
Tom commented.

"The best I have," Nate admitted.

"They say there isn't a mountain man alive who can
hold a candle to him, except maybe Jim Bridger," Milo
said.

Both men were clearly eager to meet McNair, and
Nate couldn't blame them. Shakespeare was a legend
in the Rockies, a man who had ventured into the unknown region decades ago, long before wearing beaver
became so fashionable and trappers flocked to the
mountains in droves. Shakespeare was one of the orig-
inal white inhabitants of the territory, a man whose
knowledge of the wildlife and the Indians was unsur-
passed, who knew how to hunt and trap better than
any man alive, and who spoke a dozen Indian tongues
fluently and could converse adequately in six or seven
more. The trappers in general looked up to him as a
model of what they could achieve if they tried.

Provided they lived long enough, of course. Every
mountaineer was acutely aware of the odds. Every
trapper knew that for every ten men who trekked to
the Rockies, less than half would make the return trip
one day to civilization. Most wound up slain by hos-
tiles or animals. Many simply decided to stay. There
was something about the Rockies, an indefinable qual-
ity of majesty and wonder combined with the alluring

appeal of the wild and of untrammeled freedom, that touched deep into their souls and held them as firmly as the strongest magnet held iron in its grasp.

Nate had proven susceptible to the same allure, and he didn't regret his decision to stay at all. His sojourn in the wilderness had tempered him much as a sharpening stone tempers a keen blade, dashing his boyish beliefs and his Eastern illusions on the hard rock of reality. He'd learned early that the only law that mattered in the wild was the law of the survival of the fittest. Nature played no favorites. Men and beasts must always be alert, always on their toes for trouble and ready to take advantage of situations as they developed. Those who blundered gravely seldom lived to commit the same mistake twice. If a deer didn't run fast enough from a panther, then that deer became panther food. If a man neglected to keep his rifle loaded and handy at all times and then encountered a grizzly, that man became grizzly food. It was as simple as that.

Yet despite all the latent savagery in the wilderness, despite the constant hovering overhead of the grim shadow of death ready to claim its next victim, he loved the mountains with almost as much passion as he loved Winona. He loved the regal, towering peaks crowned with snow; he loved the lush, green valleys packed with trees and verdant meadows; he loved the constant ebb and flow of the wild creatures inhabiting the Rockies, the constant swirl of life, the vibrant vitality that reached into the core of a man and made him feel truly alive.

So it was that as they rode northward, he immersed himself in the mountains, admiring the breathtaking scenery, alert for animals, keeping his mind active to take his thoughts off Winona and Zachary. They would be all right. He must trust in the Good Lord, keep his fingers crossed, and get back to them as soon as he could.

There was plenty to observe as they rode. Hawks soared by. Eagles sailed high in the sky. Ravens and mountain jays flapped overhead now and then, while smaller birds flitted about in the trees. Squirrels chattered in the high branches while chipmunks scampered on the ground. Occasionally they saw larger wildlife. Black-tailed deer were numerous. Twice they passed herds of huge elk grazing not far off. And once they saw a small herd of mountain buffalo in the brush. An enormous bull strode into the open and watched them go by but made no move to charge.

The air was crystal-clear, digging deep into the lungs with each breath and invigorating the whole body. The sky was a tranquil azure blue. A few pillowy clouds floated eastward.

"I can understand why you stay out here," Milo Benteen remarked when they were halfway to McNair's place. "If there wasn't a certain young woman waiting for me back in Pennsylvania, I'd be tempted to build a cabin and stick permanently."

"I feel the same way," Tom said. "You're fortunate, Nate, that you didn't have a woman back in the States when you came out to the frontier."

But Sublette was wrong. Nate had been close to a woman, and the statement provoked memories of the lovely Adeline Van Buren, the wealthy, prominent woman he'd intended to marry. What was she doing now? he wondered. It had been a long time since last he saw her. He'd departed New York City back in April of '28, and here it was April of '32. She must be married to a rich businessman or lawyer or politician and have children. Well, he wasn't so sure about the children, but he knew beyond any doubt that Adeline had married someone as wealthy as or wealthier than she was. Her whole life had revolved around money, no doubt because her rich father had spoiled her from childhood, had pampered her with anything and everything she wanted.

In part, Adeline was responsible for his current happiness. It had been to please her that he'd joined his Uncle Zeke and headed West. Zeke had promised to share a treasure with him, and falsely assuming Zeke had struck it rich in the fur trade or even by finding some of the vast riches in gold rumored to exist in the Rockies, he'd left New York in the expectation of returning a wealthy man and being able to marry Adeline as her social equal instead of her inferior.

Strange, sometimes, how fate worked out. The treasure his uncle had promised to share turned out to be the most precious and basic of all: simple freedom. And instead of going back to the States penniless, he'd stayed in the mountains and met a woman who surpassed Adeline in every respect, an Indian maiden who was more real woman than Adeline could ever hope to be.

He thought of Adeline from time to time. He imagined she despised him because he had gone off at such short notice with no more than a brief note of explanation. Often he wished he'd taken the time to write, to explain. But somehow he'd never been able to put his thoughts on paper.

Not even to his own family. Nate thought about them a lot too. His father, a hardworking, stern man who had not spoken about Zeke after Zeke went West, would probably never forgive Nate for doing the same. As far as his father was concerned, living in the wilderness was for fools and men who were no better than the savages they associated with.

It saddened Nate to recall his father's attitude toward the Indians. Many Easterners shared it. They regarded all Indians as savages who deserved to be driven off their lands and exterminated. Even the

President of the United States, Andrew Jackson, had publicly declared the Indians were an inferior race and should be organized as the white race saw fit.

The memory made Nate's features harden. He'd learned the truth about Indians, and he would confront any man who dared insult them in his presence. By and large, the Indians were a fine, noble people, living in harmony with the wild, and they deserved to live as they saw fit, not to have their lives dictated by those who justified bigotry in the name of patriotism.

Oh, there were bad Indians, just like there were bad whites, but the vast majority of Indians wanted much the same things longed for by the majority of whites: a family, a home, and a long life. Unfortunately, the way things were shaping up, it appeared the government wasn't going to let the Indians exist free and unmolested. Already a number of tribes living east of the Mississippi River had been forcibly uprooted and relocated. If the day ever came when the tide of white migration flowed westward past the Mississippi, the same fate might well await the Indians living on the plains and in the mountains.

Nate believed such a day was far off, if it ever occurred. Most folks in the States regarded the vast wilderness beyond the Mississippi as the Great American Desert, a name bestowed on the territory by Major Stephen Long after Long had completed a survey expedition for the government back in 1820. Except for the beaver that drew adventurous trappers to the mountains by the scores, the vast plains and the imposing Rockies held no allure for the many millions who believed the land was inhospitable and conditions unspeakably dangerous.

How wrong they were.

Nate was glad that few knew the truth. If more did, if word of the marvelous wonders and beauty to be found in the well-nigh limitless region was widely publicized, settlers would flock westward in hordes. He shuddered to think of it ever occurring. The Indian way of life, and his as well, would come to a speedy end.

Engrossed in his thoughts, he skirted a low hill and started to cross a meadow beyond. The stallion suddenly lifted its head, its ear pricked forward, and he glanced up. Hair at the nape of his neck tingled at the sight of a huge animal coming straight toward him.

It was a grizzly.

Chapter Five

Of all the wild creatures in the untamed Rockies, none were more generally feared by both whites and Indians alike than grizzlies. The mighty bears were the lords of the mountains and the plains to the east, fierce beasts that could crush the skull of a man or horse with a casual blow. Justifiably, grizzlies had earned the reputation of being extremely "hard to die," as the mountaineers liked to say. A grizzly might be shot repeatedly at close range and seemingly be unfazed by the balls or arrows.

Captains Meriwether Lewis and William Clark, on their famous expedition to the Pacific Ocean, encountered the great brutes on a number of occasions. In one particular instance, six of their best hunters decided to slay an old grizzly lying on open ground about 300 paces from a river. They snuck up on it and four men fired balls into the beast. The enraged grizzly then attacked and was shot by the other two hunters.

Unstoppable, the bear kept coming and pursued them all the way to the river, at which point it was shot again and again. When finally slain, it was on the verge of ripping one of their men to pieces. Later, when they dressed it, they found eight balls had pierced the bear, including two that had passed through the lungs and one that had broken its shoulder. Yet not until a lucky shot scored in its brain did the grizzly expire. As Lewis wrote in his journal, "These bears, being so hard to die, rather intimidate us all."

And they weren't the only ones. Nate's breath caught in his throat as he drew rein and the grizzly before them now halted, regarding them balefully. The bear was less than 50 yards away. Typical of the breed, it stood four and a half feet high at the shoulders, which were further accented by a prominent hump. This hump distinguished grizzly bears from the black variety. A large male, it easily weighed over a thousand pounds, and was capable of overtaking a horse at full gallop over a short stretch. Its brownish hairs had white tips, which gave the bear its distinctive grizzled appearance.

"Oh, Lord," Milo said softly.

Nate placed his thumb on the hammer of his rifle and waited for the bear to make the first move. If sheer savagery was their foremost trait, then being unpredictable was a close second. No one ever knew when a grizzly might charge. Sometimes a bear would spot a lone man and flee as if its hind end was on fire. At other times, a bear might encounter a party of ten or more and tear into them in unbridled fury.

This bear now reared on its hind legs to study them, its massive head swinging ponderously from side to side as it sniffed loudly. Its four-and-half-inch claws gleamed dully in the bright sunlight.

"What do we do?" Tom whispered.

"Sit tight and hope for the best," Nate advised in a low tone. "If it comes at us, scatter."

"But what about the packhorses? They can't outrun a bear loaded as they are," Tom said.

"If we scatter, it might not be able to make up its mind which one of us it wants and it will go off without chasing any of us," Nate explained, having heard of the strategy working before for the Shoshones. "If not, if it comes after any one of us, the rest can turn and help out."

The grizzly took a few lumbering strides forward, its muscles rippling under its hide.

Nate raised the Hawken. The bear had the look of one about to attack, and he wanted to get off a shot before he raced away. It would buy time for the others to put some distance between the bear and them, and might draw all of the bear's attention on himself.

Suddenly, Red Moon rode a few yards toward the bear, then stopped. His rifle resting across his thighs, he lifted both arms skyward, titled his head back, and began chanting in the Crow tongue at the top of his voice.

What was he doing? Nate wondered, watching the grizzly. Was it Red Moon's death song? He knew that warriors sometimes experienced strong premonitions of their own deaths and would sing to the spirit world before engaging in battle with enemies they believed would slay them. But he'd never heard of a brave doing so before a fight with an animal.

The grizzly cocked its enormous head back and forth, listening to the song. Then, after a minute, it sank to all fours, turned, and made for the forest at the west edge of the meadow, walking slowly, clearly unafraid yet also uninterested in conflict. In moments the murky shadows under the trees swallowed the great bear up.

Red Moon stopped chanting and took up his reins.

"Thank goodness," Tom breathed. "I thought we were in for it, there."

"Why did the bear just go away?" Milo asked.

"Who knows?" Nate responded. "Just be thankful it didn't want us for a meal." He glanced at the old Crow. "What was the song you sang, Red Moon?"

"I asked the Great Medicine Spirit for help in making the bear leave us alone," the Crow replied. "Every time I have met a grizzly, I have done the same thing and it has always worked." He paused. "My father taught me how to do it. A grizzly has not attacked anyone in our family for more winters than my people can remember."

Interesting, Nate thought. Maybe the singing had a calming effect on the bears, or maybe the grizzlies were bewildered by the songs and wanted no part of the strange singers. He goaded the stallion into a walk, pulling the pack animals behind him. "Let's go. And keep alert. Sometimes grizzlies travel in pairs."

"Hey, Red Moon," Tom said as they got underway. "If we run into the critter in this valley of yours, why don't you try singing to it to drive it off?" He winked at Milo, who chuckled.

"It would not work on the thing that lurks in the dark," the Crow answered somberly. "Nothing will."

Nate stared at the warrior. "If you're so convinced of that, why are you taking us there?"

Red Moon hesitated. "No one has ever tried to shoot the creature with a gun," he said at last. "I am hoping a ball will stop it where an arrow cannot." He gazed westward and sighed. "If not, I am an old man and have lived more winters than I should have."

"What the dickens is that supposed to mean?" Milo Benteen inquired.

"I am ready to die. There is one more task I would like to do, but if it is not meant to be, I am ready."

Milo shook his head, his eyes glittering in amusement. "No one ever *wants* to die. That's a crazy notion."

"When a man has outlived his usefulness, then it is time to go on to the spirit world," Red Moon said firmly.

"Not me," Milo said. "Death will have to take me screaming and kicking every inch of the way. I'm not about to stop breathing without a struggle."

Tom grinned, his gaze on the Crow. "I swear, if I live to be a hundred I'll never understand you Indians."

"Many of us feel the same way about you whites," Red Moon responded.

Nate laughed, although deep down he was bothered by the old warrior's attitude. There was more to Red Moon's visit to the valley of mystery than he was letting on, and Nate didn't like having the question hovering over his head, as it were, like a shadowy harbinger of trouble to come. He wanted to come right out and ask, but he'd been ingrained with the unwritten frontier edict that no man should ever pry into the personal affairs of another. He must wait until the Crow broached the subject, then take it from there.

He was extra cautious for the next mile, aware that grizzlies occasionally circled around to come at their intended victims from another direction. Only after two miles had fallen behind them did he relax completely and resume enjoying the magnificent scenery and the abundant wildlife.

They entered a long, winding valley running north and south and bore ever northward. A stream meandered on their left, gurgling softly. Now and then a fish would leap out of the water and splash down.

"Lord, these mountains are beautiful, aren't they?" Milo commented, breathing deeply.

"That they are," Nate concurred.

Tom Sublette abruptly drew rein. "What the devil

is that?" he asked, and pointed at the slope of a mountain beyond the stream.

Nate halted and looked, and right away he spotted the black shape high up on a barren part of the mountain. It was an animal, obviously, and on all fours, but the distance was too great to note specific details.

"Looks like a black wolf," Milo said. "I didn't think there was such a thing."

"No wolf," Red Moon declared. "It is a dog."

"A dog?" Tom repeated skeptically. "Where did it come from? What is it doing up there all by itself?"

"It might have strayed off from an Indian village," Nate speculated, searching the slope in the dog's vicinity. "Happens sometimes. Or there might be someone up there with it, perhaps an Indian out hunting."

"A friendly Indian?" Milo asked, shifting in his saddle and placing both hands on his rifle.

"There's no way of telling," Nate said. He clucked the stallion into motion, his eyes on the black canine. It suddenly ran into a patch of trees and was lost to view. For over a minute he watched to see if it would reappear lower down, but there was no sign of it.

"Maybe it's a stray and it will follow us," Milo said hopefully. "I wouldn't mind having a dog around. I've always liked them. Had a big hound dog when I was a kid and that critter was as loyal as could be. Saved me from a black bear once."

"If that mutt does join us," Tom stated, "you'll be the one responsible for feeding it. I'll be damned if I'm going to go out and bag game to feed a mangy, flea-ridden mongrel."

Milo gazed at him in surprise. "Don't you like dogs?"

"I'm not much on pets, period. My ma cottoned to cats and we have seven of the rascals. They were always getting their hair all over everything and none of them ever was completely housebroken."

"Cats," Milo said, and snorted. "No wonder you feel the way you do. If the Good Lord had wanted us to have cats as pets, he wouldn't have given them claws. Cats are for folks who don't know any better."

On they rode, the hours passing uneventfully. They would not reach McNair's until the next day. When there was only an hour or so until dark, Red Moon stopped once again.

"We are not alone."

Nate turned, and there was the black dog about a quarter of a mile to the rear, just standing there and staring at them. "It must be a stray," he remarked. "Milo, you might get your wish after all."

"Hold on a minute while I try to make friends," Benteen said. He started to ride toward the dog, but no sooner did he do so than the black dog whirled and darted into dense undergrowth. "Well, I'll be!" he exclaimed, reining up short. "Why did it go and do that?"

Tom chuckled. "Cats have claws and dogs don't have any brains. We'd be better off having fish as pets."

"Don't be ridiculous," Milo said. "Who ever heard of such a thing?" Reluctantly, he brought his mount around. "Well, I tried. If that dog wants to join us, the next move is up to it."

Nate glanced at the Crow, whose face was thoughtful and vaguely troubled. "Is anything wrong?" he asked.

"That dog is bad medicine. We must shoot it if we can."

Milo Benteen reacted as if he'd been slapped in the face. "What the dickens are you talking about, man?" he demanded angrily. "It's a dog, not a grizzly, and it's probably lost and hungry. I won't stand for having it shot."

Red Moon shrugged. "As you wish. But I have

warned you." He continued northward, his shoulders squared, his back stiff.

"Now you've done it," Tom groused at Milo. "You've gone and got his dander up."

"What do I care?" Milo responded. "I'm not going to let him kill an innocent dog because of some Injun drivel about bad medicine. Hell, Tom. You know as well as I do that Indians are the most superstitious bunch of people there are."

"I'll grant you that," Tom agreed. "But you shouldn't get him mad. He's the only one who knows how to find the valley. If you antagonize him, he might up and ride off one night before we get there. Then where will we be?"

Milo pondered a moment, then sighed. "All right. I'll apologize. But it galls me because I know I'm in the right." He rode faster to catch up with the old Crow.

"Yes, sir," Tom said softly more to himself than anyone else. "We can't let any harm come to that Injun until after we strike the valley."

"Or any other time," Nate said harshly. "He's in this with us all the way. And it doesn't matter if a man's companions are white or Indian, he should stick by them no matter what happens."

"Of course," Tom declared. "I didn't mean otherwise."

"I hope not," Nate said, wondering. A tiny doubt trickled into the back of his mind. Perhaps there was more to these men than met the eye. Perhaps they weren't to be trusted after all. But he promptly shook his head, discarding the suspicion as a product of his wary nature. Tom simply wanted to reach the beaver rich valley at all costs, and considering the money they stood to make from their enterprise, his attitude was understandable. Nate faced front, noting landmarks he recognized and seeking a game trail that would take them to a clearing where they could camp for the night.

"Damn. There it is again," Tom muttered.

Nate looked over his shoulder. The black dog had reappeared, still a quarter of a mile away, still following but keeping its distance, a spectral canine shadow determined to haunt their tracks for the time being. Why? What did it want? He concentrated on finding the trail, the skin between his shoulder blades itching terribly. First a grizzly, now the black dog. It was a good thing he wasn't superstitious himself, or he might be inclined to regard the two beasts as bad omens and give up on the idea of going to the valley. But the thought of all those beaver spurred him on. Nothing was going to make him change his mind: not a passing bear, not a stray dog, and certainly not an ancient legend about a creature that lurked in the dark, a creature undoubtedly long since dead.

Or so he hoped.

Chapter Six

Shakespeare McNair's cabin was situated in a pristine valley at the base of a knoll and only 50 yards from a rushing stream. To the north of the sturdily built structure was a horse pen, to the south a small storage shed. Ancient pines bordered the homestead to the rear and on both sides, while a narrow strip of ground in front of the cabin had been stripped of all vegetation. The home blended in perfectly with the surrounding vegetation. Unless one knew exactly where to look, a man could ride almost right past it without knowing it was there.

Nate wasn't certain how the mountain man would take to having three strangers show up. Nate had a standing invitation to visit any time he wanted, but Shakespeare might be upset at him for bringing the others. Many of the mountaineers were tight-lipped about the locations of their homes because they didn't want the information getting to potential enemies.

And many of the mountaineers did have bitter enemies, usually in the form of an Indian tribe that
wanted the trappers killed.

He saw no indication of activity as he approached
the closed cabin door. Maybe the grizzled codger and
his wife had gone off to visit her people, the Flathead
Indians. He scoured the ground, seeking clues, and
spied tracks that had been made within the hour.
Reining up 20 feet from the cabin, he cupped a hand
to his mouth and shouted, "Shakespeare! It's me,
Nate. Don't shoot!"

There was no reply from within.

"Perhaps he isn't home," Milo said.

"Shakespeare!" Nate repeated. "Do you hear me?"

"I hear you."

The low, gruff voice came from directly behind
them. Nate swung around, beaming happily at dis-
covering his mentor and best friend not a dozen feet
off.

As with most men who had spent any great span in
the Rockies, Shakespeare McNair look every bit as
rugged as the mountains in which he lived. Fringed
buckskins covered his muscular frame. On his head
perched a brown beaver hat, and from under the hat
spewed bushy gray hair. His beard and moustache
were the same color, testimony to his age and re-
sourcefulness in lasting as long as he had. He wore
the ubiquitous powder horn and ammunition pouch
and carried a large butcher knife on his left hip. In
his hands and pointed in the general direction of Benteen and Sublette was a cocked Hawken.

"We've come in peace, Mr. McNair," Sublette
blurted out. "Honest."

Nate was staring at the woman beside Shakespeare,
a statuesque Flathead named Blue Water Woman. She
wore a buckskin dress and held a rifle trained on Red
Moon.

"Howdy, Nate," the mountain man said cheerily, and then sobered as he regarded the pair of Pennsylvanians and the old Crow. "Where did these fellows come from?"

"They're with me," Nate explained. "My trapping partners."

"Do tell," Shakespeare said, but he made no effort to lower the gun. "I've never met any of you gentlemen before," he said to the trio. "Mind telling me your names?"

They did so, the Pennsylvanians rather nervously, the Crow smiling at some private joke.

"Obviously you know who I am," Shakespeare said, advancing slowly. Blue Water Woman stayed right by his side. "Since you're friends of Nate's, you're welcome to share my hospitality. But be forewarned." He paused and gave Benteen and Sublette long looks. "I'm a cantankerous old cuss and there are certain rules I go by. Obey them, and you won't have any trouble while you're here."

"What kind of rules?" Tom asked.

"I won't be insulted. I won't be laid a hand on. And any man who treats my wife with disrespect will be shot right then and there."

"We'd never treat your wife shabbily," Milo said indignantly. "Nor would we think of insulting you, sir. We've heard a great deal about you since we came to these parts, and we think you're one of the greatest mountaineers who has ever lived."

"Really?" Shakespeare said, a twinkle in his eyes. "Then we should get along just dandy." He lowered the Hawken, his wife lowered her rifle, and together they walked around the horses to the cabin. "Light and make yourselves to home," Shakespeare said.

Nate dismounted, ground-hitched the stallion and left the pack animals standing behind it, and walked up to his mentor. Smiling, he gave Shakespeare a clap on the shoulder. "It's good to see you again."

"Why don't you put your horses in the pen?" Shakespeare suggested.

"We're not staying that long, unfortunately," Nate responded, and squinted up at the sun, which hung high in the afternoon sky. It had taken them the better part of two days to make the journey from his cabin to McNair's. There were still five or six hours until nightfall, and he wanted to travel as far as possible before they bedded down. "The main reason I stopped by was to ask if you would check on Winona and Zach every so often until I get back."

It was Blue Water Woman who answered in her crisp, precise English. She had learned the language years ago from McNair. "We will be delighted to go see her."

"Thanks. I'm in your debt," Nate said.

"You have it backwards," Blue Water Woman responded. "It is I who am in your debt. I have not talked with another woman in over two months, and this gives me the perfect excuse to get this lazy bear to leave our cabin for a while."

"Who are you calling a lazy bear?" Shakespeare demanded.

"She'll be happy to see both of you," Nate predicted.

The mountain man watched the Pennsylvanians and Red Moon tie their animals to nearby trees. "So how did you hook up with these gents?"

Nate briefly detailed how he happened to be with his newfound acquaintances, and as he did they joined him. When he mentioned the mysterious valley ripe with beaver, Shakespeare's lake-blue eyes narrowed.

"Where is this valley?"

"Only Red Moon knows," Nate answered.

Shakespeare glanced at the Crow and addressed Red Moon in that tongue. They talked for several minutes, a frown deepening on Shakespeare's face the whole time. At last the mountain man turned to Nate.

"If you want my advice, you'll stay clear of this valley you're heading for. Going there will only bring trouble."

"Why?" Nate asked.

"It's a long story," Shakespeare said. "Why not stay for one cup of coffee at least and I'll tell you everything I know."

There was a telltale edge to McNair's tone, an edge Nate had never heard before. Was it apprehension? He nodded and said, "It's all right by me if it's all right with the others."

Milo gestured at the entrance. "Lead the way. A cup of coffee would do fine about now."

They entered, Blue Water Woman moving off to prepare the pot while the men sat down at a large round table. Shakespeare leaned back in his chair and gazed coldly at Red Moon. "I've heard about this valley before, and about the creature that supposedly lives there. These critters were common ages ago. Now they're rare."

"You know what it is?" Tom Sublette inquired dubiously.

"Not exactly," Shakespeare admitted. "There have been stories about these critters making the rounds of the camp fires for as long as I've lived in these mountains. And practically every tribe has legends about them."

"Have you ever run into one?" Milo asked.

"Nope. Thank goodness. By all accounts, you run into one and you wind up dead."

Milo smiled politely. "No offense, McNair, but my partner and I aren't given to believing every tall tale the Injuns tell. And we don't take at face value those fireside stories that are usually exaggerated ten times over."

"No offense, Benteen," Shakespeare mimicked him,

"but you haven't lived out here as long as I have. When you do, you can tell the difference between when an Indian is talking about some spirit being and when it's a real animal. And these monsters are as real as you and me."

"Monsters?" Milo repeated, and snorted. "Now I get it. You're trying to put one over on us. There are no monsters except in the minds of those fiction writers. I can read, Shakespeare, and I know about some of the books that have been so popular over in Europe and in the States. There's that strange one called *Frankenstein* by that poet's wife, and the one they made the play out of, *The Vampyre*, by that doctor. And there have been stories about those wolf-men, those werewolves, too."

Tom Sublette grinned, nodding knowingly. "And don't forget all those tales about those sea serpents off the coast of New England, and the newspaper stories about the monster that lives in Lake Erie."

"I almost forgot how you old-timers like to pull the wool over the eyes of us greenhorns," Milo said, and chuckled.

Nate saw exasperation in his mentor's eyes. He knew Shakespeare better than any man alive, and he knew when the mountain man was telling tall tales and when he was telling the truth. This bizarre business about the thing in the valley was a true story, not a whopper.

Shakespeare drummed his fingers on the table for a bit, then look at Nate. "If these two want to go off and get themselves killed, that's their business. But I've spent a lot of time teaching you everything I know, and I'd hate for you to be torn to pieces and never get to use that lore." He paused. "Are you bound and determined to go to this valley?"

"I gave them my word," Nate said.

"Damn. I wish you hadn't."

"Tell me everything you know about these critters."

"All right. The first story I know of concerns a man who explored a sizable chunk of Canada some years back. I can't recollect his name, but I know he wrote a narrative of his travels. And back in 1810 or 1811, while he was near the Athabaska River, he came on some peculiar tracks in the snow. Huge tracks, these were—"

"Probably a grizzly's," Tom interrupted.

"Since when does a grizzly have *toes*?" Shakespeare said testily, then went on. "And about fifteen years ago three men went trapping to the northwest of here. Frenchmen, they were, down from Canada. I met them at a Flathead village. They were nice enough and excited about all the game in these parts." He stopped, his gaze straying to the open door. "No one ever heard from them again, and I forgot all about them until about six years ago when I was out trapping with a gent named Rogers. We came on this old cabin, not much more than a bunch of logs set crosswise. One of the walls had been knocked down. We found old utensils and traps and such scattered about."

Nate leaned forward, fascinated. Milo and Tom were also hanging on every word.

"We found an old cap of the kind French trappers favor, about rotted through, and it reminded me of those three Frenchmen I'd met years ago. We got to poking around, and under a corner of that downed wall I noticed a bunch of bones. Wasn't much to them, but from what there was I could tell they'd been broken into bits."

"An animal, most likely," Milo said.

"No," Shakespeare stated. "These bones had been broken up when the man was still alive. Something had busted him to pieces."

No one said anything. Nate pursed his lips, pondering his course of action. He believed his friend and he believed the legends of the Indians, but he wasn't fully convinced that whatever inhabited the valley years ago still did so now, and he couldn't see breaking his word to the Pennsylvanians and calling it quits when he stood to benefit so handsomely if there were abundant beaver in the valley.

Tom coughed. "Well, let's suppose there was some kind of creature in these mountains we don't know about. What are the chances of the thing still being alive?"

Shakespeare shrugged. "Who can say?"

Milo rested his forearms on the table. "Is that all you know? Just those two stories and the Indian tales?"

"That's it," Shakespeare replied.

"We appreciate the warning, McNair, but we're not going to change our minds. We have plenty of guns. Red Moon knows the territory. And since Grizzly Killer here can kill grizzlies like most men swat flies, we don't have a blessed thing to worry about."

Nate didn't like Milo's condescending tone. Shakespeare was sincerely trying to do them a favor by emphasizing the danger and the Pennsylvanians were making light of it. "All it takes to kill a bear is a good rifle and a lot of luck. These creatures might be another story entirely."

"Now don't tell me you believe all this nonsense," Milo said. "We're counting on your experience, Nate, to help us bring in more damned beaver than most men see in two years of trapping. If you back out, we're stuck."

"I never said anything about backing out," Nate declared. "I gave you my word, and I'll stick by it."

Both Milo and Tom seemed vastly relieved. Red Moon's face was a blank stone.

Blue Water Woman brought over tin cups for each of them, then carried the pot of coffee to the table.

She poured for Shakespeare first, then for Nate.

"I am glad I heard this talk. Now I know I must stay with Winona for a long time," she commented.

"Why's that?" Nate inquired.

"I want to be there to comfort her if you do not return."

Chapter Seven

Nate pondered over the discussion at McNair's for the rest of the day, and was still contemplating his friend's words when it came time to picket the horses for the night. The four of them had ridden hard after leaving the cabin, and had not stopped until about an hour after the rosy sun sank out of sight beyond the western horizon. Since it was his turn to handle the stock, he watered the animals at a nearby stream and then found a suitable spot at the edge of the meadow where they had camped to tie the horses, allowing enough slack in the ropes to permit each horse to graze to its heart's content.

He wasn't much given to believing in spooks and goblins and such. Nor did he lend much credence to the idea of monsters existing. Unknown animals, however, were another matter. He'd seen stories back in New York about the strange creatures found by explorers in deepest Africa and in remote regions of

South America. So there probably were creatures remaining to be discovered by science, but he felt it unlikely that anything on the North American continent could still be unknown in light of the fact that adventurers, explorers, and the trappers themselves had penetrated into the heart of the Rockies and had never reported encounters with unknown beasts.

Still, there were the Indian tales and legends and they couldn't be discounted offhand. The Indians knew the land better than the whites ever would, and if the Indians believed certain creatures existed, then the odds were long that the creatures were alive or had once been.

Despite McNair's advice, he wasn't about to abandon the idea of trapping the valley. Always he came back to the same thought, that he could gather all the pelts he'd need in a short time and be back with his family much sooner than he ordinarily would at trapping season. So he decided to forge ahead and not let himself start jumping at every sound in the night.

Just as he reached his conclusion, as he turned from securing the last horse and headed for the camp fire 20 yards to the south, he heard a twig snap in the inky forest off to his right. He promptly halted and held the Hawken in both hands, peering intently into the night. The edge of the trees lay the same distance away as the fire. There was no hint of movement, but something was out there.

Nate waited, speculating it was most likely a skunk or a raccoon or some other small but harmless critter that would hasten off once it detected his scent. The large predators tended to shy away from fires, all except for wolves, and he hadn't seen any sign of a pack in the vicinity before halting to make camp. But a man could never be too careful.

Was it his imagination, or had something moved among the trunks near the meadow? He leaned forward, his thumb cocking the rifle, his finger lightly touching the cool trigger. If attacked, he must make the shot count and not fire until certain of hitting whatever came at him.

A tense minute dragged by.

Benteen and Sublette were joking and laughing by the fire, Red Moon seated across from them and not saying a word. None of them were looking in Nate's direction. He hesitated to call out and warn them for fear of appearing foolish if no threat materialized.

Another minute went by. Nate shrugged and started toward his companions. Apparently there was no cause for alarm. He took several strides, then abruptly halted as the hairs at the nape of his neck prickled and an overwhelming feeling that he was no longer alone seized him. Intuitively he sensed there was something close to him, even though he'd not heard a sound, and he swung his head around, hoping he was wrong, but knowing from prior grim experience never to discount his instincts.

Behind him, not a yard away, stood the black dog.

Startled, Nate spun and began to bring the rifle barrel up. But in his haste he tripped over his own feet and went down hard on his buttocks, the Hawken ending up in his lap. And no sooner was he on the ground and momentarily helpless than the dog closed on him.

Nate's eyes involuntarily widened as the canine stepped right up to him and stared him right in the eyes. He hadn't quite realized how big the dog was; it was immense, and even in the dark its rippling muscles were prominent. The head was huge and shaped like a box, the ears short and flopped over. The brute's eyes were uncanny, with the right one blacker than coal and the left one an unnatural shade of ivory, as if covered by a white film.

The brute's warm breath tingled Nate's nostrils and he tightened his grip on the rifle, preparing to surge to his feet and fight for his life if necessary. He was amazed the thing had been able to sneak up on him unheard and unseen, and he marveled at its prowess even as he tensed his leg muscles to stand.

Suddenly the immense dog moved, flicking its head closer and opening its gaping mouth to reveal its large, tapered teeth.

Nate flinched and tried to draw backward. He began to swing the stock, intending to bash the dog on the head. But the swing was only half completed when the animal did the unexpected.

The dog licked him.

At the clammy sensation, Nate froze, flabbergasted. He'd expected the brute to attempt to tear him to ribbons. Instead, the dog was showing him it was friendly. Again it licked him with a great roll of its wet tongue, slobbering over his face in the process. Flooded with relief, Nate began to smile and that dripping tongue slapped across his lips. He raised his right hand and wiped his sleeve across his mouth, grinning at the ridiculous situation. "That's enough, boy."

The dog recoiled at the sound of his voice, then relaxed and sat on its haunches.

Nate slowly stood. He didn't want to make any abrupt movements that might frighten the dog off, although on second thought he doubted the dog knew the meaning of fear. It was big enough to handle practically anything that came after it, standing four feet high at the shoulders and being half again as wide. He'd never seen its like anywhere and he wondered again where it came from. He'd forgotten all about it since they hadn't seen it after that first afternoon, and he'd assumed it had gone elsewhere, perhaps to an Indian encampment. "So you want some company, do you?"

The dog cocked its head and elevated its ears.

"I'm Nate King and I'm pleased to meet you," Nate

said, speaking softly to show the dog he meant no harm and could be trusted. Animals, particularly horses and dogs, usually responded remarkably well to the sound of the human voice. He'd seen a soothing tone calm the most agitated horse and pacify the most aggressive dog. So he kept talking simply to establish a rapport with it.

"I don't know where you're from or what you're doing here, but you're welcome to stay as long as you like. I like dogs myself. Had one once when I was a little boy. I reared it from a puppy and we went everywhere together until it was eight years old. Then it was run over by a wagon and killed." He stopped, saddening at the memory. "I cried for days."

The dog uttered a low whine and shifted its legs.

"Would you care for a bite to eat?" Nate asked. "We shot a buck earlier and we have plenty of meat to spare. Why don't you come along and I'll introduce you to the others." He turned slowly and motioned for the dog to follow. To his delight, the animal rose and walked on his left side, its steady gaze directed at the trio beside the fire.

Red Moon had shifted and was watching Nate and the dog approach. Sublette and Benteen had their backs to Nate and were talking about Pennsylvania.

"Gentlemen," Nate announced as he halted behind them. "We have a visitor."

"What?" Tom said, casually glancing over his left shoulder. The dog's huge face was inches from his own, its eerie eyes unblinking and hard, and he yelped in astonishment, leaping to his feet. "What the hell!"

"Well, I'll be!" Milo exclaimed, smiling and rising. "I never expected to see you again, boy," he said, extending a hand to pat the dog on the head.

To Nate's surprise, the dog uttered a rumbling growl, its lips curling back from its teeth. For a moment he thought the dog would snap at Milo's fingers and he quickly said, "No! Behave yourself!"

The dog glanced up at him, then ceased growling and stood still.

"He seems to have taken a liking to you," Milo observed, slowly withdrawing his hand.

"I hope you don't intend to keep it," Tom stated. "We'll have enough to do without having to take care of a dumb mongrel."

"I suspect this dog can take care of itself," Nate commented, stepping up to the fire to take a seat. The dog stayed by his side and sat down when he did.

"Well, I don't like it," Tom persisted. "And since I have a one-fourth interest in this enterprise, I think I have a say in whether the dog stays or goes. And I vote it goes."

"Be reasonable, Tom," Milo said. "What harm can it do to have the dog come along?"

"That thing just growled at you and you still want to keep it around?" Sublette responded.

"I like dogs. You know that. And I vote the dog can stay if it wants," Milo said.

Nate looked at the old Crow, recalling what Red Moon had said about the dog being bad medicine. "How about you? What do you say?"

The warrior stared silently at the dog for a full minute before finally answering. "Our paths are now joined for better or for worse. Do as you want."

"What the hell is that supposed to mean?" Tom asked.

"It means the dog stays," Nate declared, and reached over to scratch it under the chin. The dog didn't growl or make any threatening moves. "Since I'm the one it has attached itself to, I'll be responsible for it."

Tom scowled, moved a few feet away, and sat down. "Next we'll be taking in stray grizzly cubs," he grumbled.

Leaning forward, Milo whispered to Nate. "Pay no attention to him. He's just in one of his moods. By tomorrow morning he'll have a whole new disposition." Straightening, he joined his friend.

The buck slain earlier had been butchered by Red Moon and chunks of roasting meat were now suspended over the fire on a crude spit. Nate drew his butcher knife and sliced off a small section that was still quite rare, then offered it to the dog. Although he held the meat right next to its nose, the dog showed no interest.

"That's odd," Milo remarked. "I never knew a dog to refuse meat before."

"Maybe it ate a while ago and isn't hungry," Nate speculated, placing the morsel at the dog's feet in case it should change its mind. The dog rose, took a step sideways, and laid down with its head resting on its forepaws. The flickering firelight played over the animal's sleek black coat, and when Nate gazed at its back he noticed a series of long, jagged lines crisscrossing its hide from the top of its neck to well past its shoulders. Curious, he placed his right hand on its neck and the dog flinched and raised its head to give him a quizzical stare. He suddenly realized what the lines were. "This dog is covered with scars."

Milo came over and studied them. "It looks as if someone beat him with a whip clear down to the bone. Not once, but a lot of times." He shook his head in disgust. "No wonder this dog isn't too fond of people."

The scars were old. Nate guessed the whippings had taken place well over a year ago, if not longer, and he reasoned that a white man must have been responsible. Indians rarely beat their dogs. Oh, they might smack one with a stick if it misbehaved badly, but if a dog was a chronic troublemaker they simply ate it.

"Maybe he was with another party of trappers and ran off after being mistreated," Milo said.

That could well be, Nate reflected. Trappers, by and large, were drinking men. And when under the influence of demon alcohol, their tempers could flare mightily. Men who wouldn't hurt a soul when sober might turn into hateful brutes when drunk. He'd once seen a drunken trapper beat a fine horse to within an inch of its life, and when the man had sobered up he'd bawled like a child over what he'd done.

"What do you figure to call it?" Milo asked.

"I don't know," Nate said. He hadn't given a name much thought.

"How about Blackie?"

Nate gazed at the dog, at its powerful build, and said, "How about Samson?"

"Samson?" Milo repeated, and glanced at the animal. "Why not? It sure fits him. He's got more muscles than any dog I've ever known. I like it."

"Who cares what you call it?" Tom Sublette said, and looked at the Crow. "Let's discuss something really important. I, for one, would like to know how long it will take us to reach the valley."

"It was agreed you would not question me about the valley before we get there," Red Moon said.

"I'm not asking for a detailed map," Tom said sharply. "But it would help if we knew how long the trip will take."

Red Moon pondered a bit. "Very well. It will take nine sleeps, possibly ten."

Ten days of hard riding? Nate scratched his chin. That would put them close to Blackfoot country, all right. And if the Blackfeet found them, their scalps might end up hanging in a warrior's lodge. He thought of Winona and Zach and hoped he wasn't making the biggest mistake of his life.

Far off, a wolf howled.

Chapter Eight

For five days they pushed in a generally northwestern direction, skirting ragged peaks and high country lakes, wisely staying off of ridges and hills and any other elevated points where they ran the risk of sky-lining themselves. Twice they saw the smoke of camp fires, but uncertain of the identity of those who made the fires and the reception they might receive should they venture too near, they shied away from making contact.

Wildlife was everywhere. Majestic elk and alert deer, shaggy buffalo and lumbering bears, soaring birds of prey and chattering chipmunks.

The sky was a deep blue, the clouds fluffy and white as they drifted overhead. The air invigorated the lungs.

Nate drank in the sights, sounds, and smells, as he always did, his soul vibrant with the pulse of life. He'd watch mountain sheep perched on narrow trails thousands of feet up leap from one precarious foothold to another and marveled at their dexterity. He'd watch a bald eagle execute a lightning dive to snatch an unwary rabbit and had been amazed at the eagle's speed and accuracy.

This was the life for him. No matter how long he stayed in the rugged Rockies, he would never tire of the beauty and wonder all around him. Occasionally he would think about New York and his parents, and he knew deep down that he would never return there to live. A visit, though, might be in order, if only to let his folks see his son and meet his wife. But that was a matter to ponder at length later, after trapping season.

His newfound canine companion stayed by him nearly all the time. The dog never barked. It never displayed the slightest fear of the horses, nor did it display concern when they sighted wandering grizzlies. And it never begged for food. When they stopped for meals the dog sat silently besides Nate and refused meat and drink.

"It's downright spooky the way this critter behaves," Tom mentioned on the fourth day. "I've never heard tell of a dog that didn't eat before."

But Nate knew better. Two or three times a day the dog would dash off into the brush and be gone for anywhere from thirty minutes to an hour. Eventually, inevitably, it would catch up with them again and take its position near his horse. Where it went he could only guess. Several times he noticed drops of dried blood or bits of fur on its chin, and he deduced it was going off regularly to hunt its own game and drink. For whatever reason, the dog would accept food from no man.

Sublette complained now and again about the dog being along. He would sarcastically remark that they could always eat it if they ran short of provisions.

Milo tried to befriend the dog, but was rebuffed every time.

And Red Moon neither made comments nor tried to get the dog to like him. Often, at night, he would sit and watch it, his brow furrowed, never revealing the trail his thoughts were following.

Then, on the fifth night, an incident occurred that drastically changed Tom Sublette's opinion.

They had camped at the base of a cliff where the towering rock wall shielded them from the wind and a convenient spring provided cold water. That afternoon Nate had shot a black-tailed deer, and he was roasting juicy steaks over the fire while Milo took care of the horses, Tom gathered wood for the fire, and Red Moon stood and stared at the sky.

"There will be heavy rain tomorrow," the Crow announced after a while.

"Shouldn't slow us up much," Nate said conversationally, and flipped over one of the steaks in the pan. Beside him, as always, was Samson.

"We are making good time," Red Crow said. "Four more sleeps and we will be at the valley."

Nate saw an opening and took advantage. "I hope there are still plenty of beaver there. My wife and I could use the money from the sale of our peltries to take a trip back to the States. How about you?"

Red Crow was silent for a bit. "I need my share of the money for my grandson."

"Planning to buy him a whole herd of fine horses?" Nate joked.

"No. I want to take him to a white doctor in St. Louis."

About to flip another steak, Nate stopped, the knife poised in his right hand. "A doctor? What's wrong with the boy?"

"He was climbing a tree fourteen moons ago when he fell and landed on rocks. Since then he has not been able to walk. Our medicine men have tried every cure they know but nothing has worked. They say the boy might never walk again."

The sorrow in the old warrior's voice touched a responsive chord in Nate. "You must love him very much."

"Little Sparrow is the joy of my life. I want him to grow to be a great warrior," Red Moon said softly. "All my other grandchildren are girls." He shook his head in disappointment. "My sons must not be living right."

The idea of an Indian visiting a doctor was a new one to Nate. He knew many tribes sent members to St. Louis to trade or to meet with the Superintendent of Indian Affairs. Where medicine was concerned, though, Indians preferred their customary treatments to the strange practices of the whites.

"I was told about your doctors from a trapper friend," Red Moon revealed. "He said they know very little of the many plants that can heal the sick and they never use a sweat lodge, but somehow they still manage to cure those who come to them. It is most puzzling."

Nate turned the second steak over.

"I do not know if a white doctor can help my grandson, but I will take him there to find out. I must try every way I can," Red Moon said. "My friend told me white doctors take money for their treatments, much money sometimes. Now you know why I need my share, and why I will work very hard to make sure we catch as many beaver as we can."

Indeed, Nate reflected. And he knew much more. Such as why Red Moon was willing to violate a tribal taboo and take them to the remote valley, even though the Crow must be deathly afraid of encountering the creature his tribe so dreaded. The trip to St. Louis was an act of desperation on Red Moon's part, his last hope to cure his grandson.

Milo walked up. "Got the horses settled down for the night," he mentioned. "What were you two talking about?"

"We were making small talk," Nate said, and saw Tom approaching with broken branches for the fire.

Samson growled.

Nate glanced at the big dog, thinking it was growling at Tom. Instead, Samson was peering into the forest to the southeast, his lips trembling in anger, his eyes narrowed.

"He must hear something," Milo said.

Rising, Nate stood with the knife in one hand and the pan in another, listening to the night sounds. Or trying to. Because he suddenly realized the forest ringing their camp had grown totally silent. Even the insects were still. Not so much as a cricket chirped.

Tom edged backwards toward the fire. "What is it? What's out there?"

Before Nate could answer, Samson streaked into the vegetation, gliding like a living shadow into the Stygian darkness of the wilderness. "No," Nate said, to no avail. Placing the pan down, he slid the knife into his sheath and scooped up his Hawken. Fixing on the point where Samson had entered the trees, he trotted toward it.

"Wait! Where are you going?" Milo called out.

"To see what's out there," Nate responded. "Stay here until I get back."

"Don't—" Milo objected.

But Nate had already plunged into the murky realm that constituted the forest at night. He went several yards, then halted and crouched to get his bearings and listen. What had the dog heard or scented? A bear? A panther? Wolves? Or other men? He doubted it had been Indians since Indians rarely were abroad after the sun set. Few raids were conducted at night, for the simple reason that many tribes believed the souls of those slain at night were fated to aimlessly wander the earth and never attain the Indian version of heaven.

He heard nothing himself, but that meant nothing. The dog's hearing undoubtedly was much sharper than his. There must be something in the woods nearby to account for the dog's agitation, and he wanted to find whatever was out there before whatever was out there found them.

Then, from the southeast, there came the faintest whisper of sound.

What had it been? Nate strained his ears, trying to identify the vague noise. More than anything else, it had sounded like the tip of a limb brushing against buckskin clothing. He went deeper into the woods, staying low, using every bush and tree for cover, his moccasins making no noise as he moved. His years spent in the wilderness had honed his woodsman skills to perfection. In many respects he was much like an Indian, and some might say he was more Indian now than white. Which wouldn't bother him in the least. He'd take it as a compliment.

After traveling 40 yards from the camp, he still saw no reason for the dog's behavior. He stopped beside a wide tree, gazing in all directions, and detected movement at the limits of his vision. Sliding behind the trunk, he held the rifle firmly and waited.

Soon he heard them: Indians, sneaking toward the campfire, making barely any noise, but enough for him to tell who was approaching. The pad of stealthy feet, of men moving quickly in the direction of the fiery glow at the base of the cliff, alerted him to the fact there were at least four or five and they were on both sides of him.

His back flush to the tree, crouching as low as he

could, Nate placed his thumb on the hammer and froze. Could they be Crows? This was Crow territory. If so, they would probably be friendly and he didn't want to shoot them without provocation.

To the right a black form materialized, then a second. To the left appeared three more. They were concentrating on the fire to the exclusion of all else and none, evidently, looked in Nate's direction. He saw them advance less than ten feet and halt. One of the men whispered to another, the words barely audible.

Was that the Crow tongue? Nate wondered. He didn't think so but he couldn't be certain. Peering through the trees, he saw Milo and Tom near the fire with their rifles in their hands. Red Moon was not in sight. If these Indians were hostile, and if he let them get any closer to the camp, they'd be able to easily pick the two Pennsylvanians off before Benteen and Sublette knew what hit them. He couldn't let that happen.

Easing lower, hoping his figure would be indistinguishable against the background, Nate spoke clearly. "Who are you and what do you want?"

His words sparked swift reaction. An Indian on the left wheeled and a rifle boomed, the muzzle spitting flame and lead.

Nate heard the ball smack into the tree above his head. The other Indians were scattering. He sighted on the one who had fired, who seemed to be trying to reload, and let the Hawken show how much he appreciated being shot at. At the retort from his gun, the Indian shrieked in pain and fell. Instantly, Nate dived to the right, and it was well he did.

Two other guns spoke, and two more balls struck the trunk of the tree.

Rolling to one knee, Nate held the rifle in his left hand and drew one of his flintlocks with his right. He cocked the hammer as he drew so he was set to fire when his arm reached full extension. Only there were no targets to shoot at. The four remaining Indians had gone to ground.

Realizing they would be out for his blood, Nate crept to the right. A stationary target was a sitting duck. He must keep constantly on the move if he hoped to partially counter their numerical advantage.

Off to the left there was an abrupt screech, then total silence.

What had that been all about? Nate mused, easing flat in the shelter of a low thicket. He crawled to his right, wishing he could reload the Hawken but knowing he increased his risk if he did. If they converged on him he had his two pistols and his butcher knife, and they would learn the hard way that a King was as hard to kill as the mighty bears after which he had been named.

A commotion erupted and Nate heard much thrashing and flailing. The scuffle was punctuated by the low growl of a beast and the strangled cry of a man. Suddenly, quiet descended once more.

Had that been Samson? Nate continued to crawl, scouring the ground. He hoped Benteen and Sublette would have the good sense not to blunder into the forest bellowing his name. By now they should have taken cover.

A second commotion ensued, much louder than the first, and the growling was much more ferocious. No one screamed, but a few seconds after the noise stopped, someone groaned in acute agony.

What the blazes was going on out there? Nate wondered as he skirted the end of the thicket, trying to outflank the Indians on the right. His elbow struck a thin dead branch lying on the ground and it broke with a sharp crack.

Fuming at his stupidity, Nate rose into a crouch and dashed to the right. The Indians were bound to have heard and would easily pinpoint his position. He must put distance behind him or find a hiding place.

One moment he was adroitly weaving among the trees, the next someone hurtled out of the night and slammed into him from the rear. He was knocked forward, onto his knees, and when he frantically twisted to see his attacker he saw a tall warrior armed with a knife—a knife that streaked at his face.

Chapter Nine

In sheer desperation, Nate threw himself to the right. He felt the tip of the blade dig into his left shoulder, felt a clammy sensation as blood spurted over his skin, and then he was on his back with his attacker looming above him in the dim light, ready to stab again. His right arm jerked the pistol straight out and he fired at close range into the Indian's abdomen.

The force of the ball made the warrior stagger backwards and the man doubled over, let go of his knife, and clutched at his stomach.

Nate pushed off the ground, stuck the spent pistol under his belt, and drew his second flintlock. It wasn't needed, though. The warrior was doubled over, his forehead resting on the grass, groaning pitiably. The knife lay at his feet.

Taking no chances, Nate backpedaled a few feet and covered the man. Suddenly, from out of nowhere, appeared Red Moon. The Crow slipped up beside Nate and stared at the downed warrior, who had tilted his head to peer at them.

"Blackfeet," he commented.

"This far south?" Nate responded absently while gazing anxiously around for sign of the rest.

"They go where they please, when they please. These must have been looking for a village to raid when they saw our fire."

"There were five in all," Nate informed him, looking over his shoulder.

"I know. Now there is just this one."

The man on the ground spoke, uttering his few words defiantly.

"He speaks my tongue," Red Moon said. "He says all Crows are cowards and fit for the buzzards."

Nate was worried about the remaining Blackfeet. He expected one of them to charge or open fire at any second. "What about the others?"

"Dead."

"All of them?"

"Yes," Red Moon said, and tapped the knife he wore on his left hip. "I killed one. You shot one with your rifle and then this one. And the dog sent the last two to meet their ancestors."

"Samson?"

"Is there another dog around here?"

Nate turned in time to see the big black beast advance out of a tangle of vegetation nearby. Samson strolled over to him and stood at his side, staring wickedly at the wounded Blackfoot brave. He thought the dog might tear into the man and said sternly, "No. Leave him alone." He had no idea if Samson understood, but the dog made no move toward the warrior.

Crashing in the underbrush heralded the arrival of Benteen and Sublette, who hurried over with their rifles at the ready.

"Who is he, Nate?" Milo asked, gesturing at the brave.

"What happened?" Tom added. "We heard shooting and growling and such."

"This here is a Blackfoot," Nate informed them. "He and his friends were fixing to take our scalps."

"Blackfeet!" Milo exclaimed. Like every other trapper in the Rockies, he'd heard all about the many white men slain by the fierce tribe. "How many were there?"

"Five."

Tom glanced at Samson. "Well, I'll be damned! This mutt of yours saved our bacon by hearing them before they could get close enough to put an arrow or a ball into us."

"That he did," Nate agreed.

"If you want to keep him, I won't raise a ruckus," Tom said.

"What about this one?" Milo inquired, jabbing his rifle at the brave at their feet. "Shouldn't we finish him off?"

As if the Blackfoot understood, he came up in a rush, his bloody arms flashing out with the knife clutched in his right hand. He tried to stab Red Moon in the neck, but the wily Crow was a shade faster and sidestepped.

Nate pivoted, bringing his flintlock to bear, but before he could fire there was a tremendous snarl and Samson sprang like a pouncing panther. The big dog didn't bother going for an arm or leg as would others of his kind. Samson went straight for the throat, his momentum and weight enabling him to sweep past the Blackfoot's knife and knock the brave over. They went down, Samson on top, his teeth sunk deep in the Blackfoot's soft neck.

Still game, the Blackfoot drew back his knife arm to stab Samson in the side. Nate saw the movement and tramped down hard on the brave's forearm with his foot, pinning the arm and the knife in place. He held his leg firm as the Blackfoot gurgled and thrashed, listening to the slurping sounds made by Samson as the dog's teeth shredded the Blackfoot's throat. A whine rent the cool air, not the low whine of a dog but the terrified whine of a man who was dying, a man who fought and struggled with all his waning strength but was no match for the massive brute chewing his neck to bits.

Abruptly, the Blackfoot lay still.

Samson moved back, blood dripping from his muzzle. Tiny pieces of pale flesh dotted his cheeks and lined his mouth.

"If I ever forget myself and try to kick this mongrel," Tom said softly, "I want somebody to shoot me before it can get to me."

"Consider it done," Milo said, grinning.

Red Moon drew his knife. "I claim the scalp of the man I killed, but the rest are yours, Grizzly Killer."

"Mine?" Nate repeated distastefully. Of the few Indian practices he disliked, scalping was at the top of his list. He'd taken the hair of a few foes since arriving in the Rockies, but he couldn't reconcile his conscience to the horrid practice.

"You shot one and your dog finished off the rest," Red Moon stated. "So, by right, four of the scalps are yours."

"I don't want them," Nate said.

"You're passing up four fine scalps?" Milo asked in astonishment.

"When you've taken as many as I have, what's one more?" Nate said as nonchalantly as he could.

"I'd hate to see them go to waste," Milo said, looking down at the last Blackfoot.

"If you want them, they're yours."

"What about me?" Tom interjected. "I've never taken a scalp either, and I wouldn't mind having the hair of a Blackfoot hanging from my belt."

"Divide them, then," Nate proposed. "Each of you can have two."

"You really mean it?" Milo responded eagerly.

"Yes."

"You're all right in my book." Tom beamed, drawing his knife. "It takes a big man to share scalps. Wait until we tell everyone about this. You'll be the talk of the mountains."

"I'd prefer if you didn't tell a soul," Nate said.

"If that's what you want," Tom said, and knelt to grip the Blackfoot's shoulder-length black hair.

Nate didn't stay to see the scalps removed. He started toward their camp, appalled by the attitude of the Pennsylvanians. Then he reminded himself that many trappers shared the same attitude, and some could boast of having a dozen or more scalps in their possession. For that matter, the Indians were no better. Every male in every tribe prided himself on his bravery in battle and the number of coups he'd counted. Owning a string of scalps conferred great prestige on the warrior who did, and Indian men entertained no qualms about lifting hair.

He was pouring hot coffee into his tin cup when the others drifted back. Red Moon had the fresh scalp attached to his thin leather belt. Milo held two in his hand and was examining them critically. Tom Sublette was swinging his and chuckling like a giddy child who had just received a new toy.

"Wait until I show these to the folks back in Pennsylvania," Tom declared happily. "Why, they'll think I'm the greatest Injun-fighter since Daniel Boone."

"But you didn't kill those Indians," Milo noted.

Tom laughed and winked. "We know that, but my friends in Pennsylvania won't." He swung the scalps again and grinned.

"Boone would roll over in his grave," Milo said.

"He'd understand," Tom countered. "After all, Boone was born in Pennsylvania just like we were." He paused. "Besides, it's just in the nature of a practical joke. I'm not trying to hurt anyone."

Nate had heard all he could abide. "A man should never claim credit for a killing that isn't properly his," he commented, and took a sip of the delicious, steaming coffee.

"It's easy enough for you to criticize me," Tom said resentfully, "when you already have a reputation the likes of which most men only dream about." He snorted. "You're the mighty Grizzly Killer who can slay grizzlies with his bare hands. You can track and shoot as good as any Indian who ever lived. Beaver drop dead at the mere mention of your—"

"That will be enough!" Nate snapped, rising.

The others froze. They all knew there were certain things a man never did when in the company of others. A man never asked prying questions because many men had left the States to escape pasts they would rather forget. A man never made fun of another man's woman because there was no surer way of getting a fist in the face. And a man never, ever insulted another man or treated others sarcastically unless he was ready to back his foolishness with a knife or a gun.

"We're trapping partners, but that doesn't give you the right to treat me like a green pilgrim," Nate said sternly. "Any reputation I have, I've earned the hard way."

Tom glowered for a full ten seconds. Only when Milo said softly "Tom" did he glance at Benteen and then sigh. He faced Nate. "All right. I was wrong and I admit it. Sorry, King."

"No harm done," Nate responded, and squatted in front of the fire. In his heart, though, he was developing a dislike for Tom Sublette. The man had a high regard for himself and a low regard for others, a dangerous combination in any person. Nate almost wished he'd had the presence of mind to turn down their offer, but again he thought of all the furs he would collect and of getting back to the cabin much earlier than he normally would. He would just have to put up with Sublette's behavior for a few months.

Milo, who was tying his scalps to his belt, suddenly looked up. "Say, I just had a thought. What if those shots were heard by other Indians?"

"They might have been," Red Moon said.

"We'll act on the assumption someone did hear them," Nate said. "And since we're avoiding other company for the time being, we'll saddle up and cut out of here before first light. If someone comes to investigate tomorrow morning, we'll be long gone before they find where we've camped."

"I will keep first watch," Red Moon volunteered.

"I'll go second," Nate said, and drank more coffee while listening to Milo and Tom argue over who should pull guard duty third and fourth. At times they were more like bickering boys than full-grown men.

He sipped again, pondering. What had happened to him? he wondered. There had been a time when they wouldn't have bothered him in the least, not even Sublette. There had been a time when others could tease him and he would have merely laughed and gone about his business. Why, now, was he so different?

All of the old-timers he knew were the same way. By old-timer, he meant anyone who had lived in the Rockies for more than two or three years. In comparison to the number of men who flocked to the Rockies to trap, very few stayed on for long. Most died, either from Indians, beasts, or accidents. Men like Shakespeare McNair and Jim Bridger were the exceptions rather than the rule. And they too were touchy about being offended.

Why? And when had he changed and become like them? What had done it?

Was it because living in the wilderness, where a person encountered the majesty of creation on a daily basis, conferred a profound sense of inner dignity on those who did so? A dignity above reproach, but not above reprimanding those who belittled it?

Was it because living in the wilderness, where survival was often won by superior wits and endurance, made a person appreciate his or her own uniqueness that much more, made a man realize he was special and had a place in the greater scheme of things? Consequently, he was unwilling to abide the insults of those who didn't know any better?

Or was the cause simpler than that? Was it because the wilderness took a man and molded his soul in its own hard image? Nature, after all, was never forgiving or compassionate. Everywhere, the strong prayed on the weak. The slow deer fell to the panther, the weak elk was taken by wolves. And men who were weak seldom lasted out a year in the wild Rockies. Only the hard ones lived on. Those who were living reflections of the life-and-death spectacle surrounding them.

Nate shook his head, clearing his mind, and smiled at himself over his train of thought. He was starting to think in circles, just like Shakespeare often did. Give him another five years and he'd probably wind up as crotchety as that cantankerous old cuss!

"I hope we don't run into any more Blackfeet before we reach the valley," Milo was saying.

"The valley is very close to Blackfoot country," Red Moon reminded him. "Very close. We must be on our guard at all times. But if we are careful, we will have much money when it is all over."

"Now you're talking, Injun," Tom said. "I can't wait to hold a couple of thousand dollars in my hand. I've never had that much money at one time."

"Do not forget a share goes to me," Red Moon said.

Tom glanced sharply at the Crow. "I won't forget, old man. Don't you worry none. And don't you forget that for you to collect your money, we've got to make it back alive."

Nate took a long swallow and peered at his companions over the rim of his cup, speculating on how many would actually make it back.

Only time would tell.

Chapter Ten

"The valley," Red Moon said, and pointed straight ahead.

Nate placed a hand on the pommel and leaned forward to survey the land before them. They had reined up in a small clearing on a pine-covered ridge, and it became immediately apparent why few knew the location of the valley.

The old Crow had led them into stark, rugged country rarely visited by human beings. Regal mountains were everywhere, most craggy peaks over ten thousand feet high. Between and among the mountains were deep gorges, steep ravines, and occasional verdant valleys. Many were dead ends. The whole area was like a gigantic maze carved by the erratic hand of the whimsical elements.

The ridge on which they had stopped bordered an isolated series of jagged spires and rocky heights that formed a seemingly impassable barrier. Situated as it was so close to those heights, the ridge cut off from view whatever lay at their base. And there, nestled between two mountains looming over 12 thousand feet above the ground, was the opening to a lush valley.

"Well, I'll be damned," Milo commented. "We're finally here."

"Where the hell are we?" Tom wanted to know, and shot a questioning look at Nate.

"It's a branch of the Rockies, but I don't know which one," Nate said. "I've never been this far northwest before." He paused. "Very few have."

"What are we waiting for?" Milo asked eagerly, and nodded at the valley entrance. "Let's get down there and set up camp for the night."

Nate took the lead, squinting up at the late afternoon sun. There were about four hours of daylight remaining, enough for them to find a suitable spot to bed down. Bright and early tomorrow morning they could scout the valley and see if the beaver were as abundant as Red Moon had claimed.

He glanced over his shoulder at the warrior, who was riding at the rear of the line, and noticed Red Moon cast an anxious gaze toward the two mountains flanking the valley. Was the Crow thinking about the thing that lurked in the dark? Or about the Crow braves who had gone into the valley and never emerged? Facing front, Nate placed the Hawken across his thighs so he could lift it quickly in an emergency.

All around was wildlife. There were hawks high above them, ravens and jays in the trees. Chipmunks darted from under rocks and squirrels chattered from the treetops. Elk and deer prints were plentiful.

Nate saw no reason to be alarmed. With so much game there must be few predators in the area. Once, at the bottom of the ridge, he spied a bear track, but it was that of a black bear and not a grizzly.

They rode to the opening, a relatively narrow gap between the mountains, no more than 50 feet wide. Pines grew in profusion on both sides of a broad stream that flowed out of the gap and angled abruptly to the left, to the west. The stream flowed along the base of the peaks for hundred of yards, then disappeared in deep forest. From the ridge the stream had not been visible because of the high grass and weeds that grew along each bank and the overhanging branches of the many trees bordering the slowly flowing water.

"This is right pretty," Milo said.

Nate nodded in agreement. The countryside was picturesque. If the valley wasn't so close to Blackfoot territory, it would be an ideal spot to build a cabin and raise a family. He goaded his stallion through the gap, sticking to the east bank of the stream, listening to the gurgling water and the soft wind whispering in the branches.

"Say, look there!" Tom exclaimed, pointing.

At that moment Nate saw it too: a large beaver dam constructed from reeds, saplings, sticks, and branches all woven into a compact mass and caulked with mud. Past the damn, in an oval pond, was the beaver lodge, a dome of similar construction well over seven feet high and 30 feet wide, average size. There were no beaver in evidence, but it was still early. Mainly active at night, beaver usually made their appearance in the early evening.

"That's a good sign," Milo said. "Where there's one lodge there might be a lot more."

Similar thoughts inspired Nate. They had barely entered the valley and already found a lodge. It had been his experience that the farther up a valley a trapper went, the more lodges and beaver he would find.

And so they did. They passed dam after dam, lodge

after lodge, and twice saw beaver swimming. The animals paid no attention to them, which in itself was promising because it meant the beaver had had few dealings if any with hunters or trappers and would be easier to catch.

The valley stretched on for mile after mile, widening out as they advanced, winding between magnificent peaks to the east and the west. At its widest the valley covered five to six miles. Occasionally it narrowed to only two miles or less. Small herds of elk and black-tailed deer were frequently spotted. At various points they came on tributaries of the main stream, creeks branching off to the right or the left, and they saw beaver dams and lodges up those too.

Milo laughed lightly. "I think I've died and gone to trappers' heaven."

"I've never seen so many beaver in one valley before," Tom said. "How about you, Nate?"

"Me neither," Nate admitted.

Tom looked at Red Moon. "I've got to hand it to you, old man. You were right. You knew what you were talking about."

"We will catch many beaver," the Crow predicted.

They hadn't gone more than a third of the way into the valley when Nate decided to call a halt. The sun perched low on the western mountains and would soon drop from view, plunging the valley into deep shadows and eventual darkness. He studied those jagged peaks, realizing they cut off the sunlight much earlier than would normally be the case. He estimated night fell in the valley a good half hour before it did, say, at his cabin.

Nate picked a spot where a meadow bordered the main stream as their campsite. While Tom got a fire going and Red Moon gathered dead wood, Nate and Milo stripped the horses and took them to the stream to drink. Samson stayed near Nate.

"This valley is better than I'd dare dream," Milo mentioned, beaming as he surveyed the expanse still before them. "If all goes well, I'll return to Pennsylvania with enough money to put down on a sizable farm. Maggie will be so happy. I gave her a ring before I left for these mountains. Hope she hasn't grown tired of waiting for me."

"I wish the two of you the best."

They tethered the horses in the meadow, then strolled to the fire, where a pot of coffee was already boiling. Red Moon had taken a seat and was chewing on a piece of jerked meat.

"I can hardly wait to start trapping," Tom said as he poured coffee into Nate's cup.

"We have a few things to do before we trap," Nate told him. "We should go to the end of the valley and see if there are a lot of beaver farther up. Then we can pick our first camp and begin to set traps."

"First camp?" Milo repeated.

"This valley must be twenty-five to thirty miles long," Nate said. "If we were to set up a permanent camp near the center, whoever went out to check the traps couldn't possibly make it back by dark and would have to bed down in the brush. It's too far to cover from end to end at one time. So I propose trapping one section of the stream at a time and working our way down the valley until we're done. We can move our camp farther down as we go along so each of us won't have as far to travel when we check the trap lines."

"Makes sense to me," Milo said.

"Me too," Tom added.

Red Moon, who was bearing more wood to the fire, halted and said, "There is more to this valley."

"What do you mean?" Milo responded.

"The valley forks far up. There is another part as long as this one."

"Does it have as many beaver?" Milo asked.

"More," the Crow answered, and deposited his load of wood.

Tom laughed and slapped his thigh in delight. "This is too good to be true. We don't have enough pack animals for all the pelts we'll collect."

"When will we reach the fork?" Nate wanted to know.

"Well after the sun is straight overhead we should be there," Red Moon informed him.

Because they had not shot any game, they had to make do with jerky and biscuits Milo made from the flour in their provisions. Hot coffee capped off their meal. Then they settled around the fire and discussed their trapping plans.

"Should we take turns standing guard?" Tom inquired at one point.

"There is no need," Red Moon said.

"What about the Blackfeet?" Tom mentioned. "You keep telling us that we're close to their country."

"The Blackfeet do not come into this valley."

Nate, about to take a sip, stopped and studied the Crow's impassive features. "Why not?"

"For the same reason my people no longer come here," Red Moon said.

Milo snickered. "Are you saying the Blackfeet are also afraid of this thing that lurks in the dark?" He shook his head in disbelief. "The Blackfeet don't know the meaning of fear."

"They do not come here," Red Moon reiterated.

Swallowing more coffee, Nate gazed into the inky night. Like Milo, he was skeptical. The Blackfeet deserved their reputation for being indomitable warriors. They fought everyone and everything. Even grizzlies didn't intimidate them. So why would they shun this valley when it was a hunter's paradise?

"Now don't start with that nonsense again," Tom

grumbled. "We haven't seen anything unusual since we got here. And I don't recollect any of us seeing so much as a strange track."

"Once the creature knows we are here, it will come," Red Moon stated. He removed a piece of jerky from his pack and took a bite.

"There is no damned creature," Tom insisted. "And I don't want to hear you talk of it again."

"As you wish."

A nervous whinny suddenly issued from one of the packhorses, and a moment later several others had chimed in with loud whinnies of their own.

"What the hell?" Tom blurted.

Nate grabbed his Hawken, rose, and hurried toward the stock. Perhaps because of the fireside conversation, his every nerve was on edge. On his left was Samson, not displaying any agitation whatsoever. Red Moon and Milo were on the right. Nate reached the tethered animals and saw them staring intently to the northeast with their ears pricked.

"There is something out there," Milo whispered.

But what? Nate wondered, his thumb on the hammer of his rifle. They couldn't afford to lose any of their animals. They only had one riding horse apiece, and the eight packhorses would be sorely needed to transport the furs.

Then, from perhaps half a mile away, a piercing shriek rent the cool air, a shriek resembling that of a terrified woman in agonizing torment. The horses fidgeted anxiously, a few tugging on their ropes.

Milo lowered his rifle and snorted. "It's just a panther. The stock must have picked up its scent."

"What if it tries to get one of our horses?" Tom asked from behind them.

"Perhaps we should post guards after all," Nate suggested. "I'll take the first watch if no one has any objections."

No one did. They walked back to the fire. Nate finished his coffee while standing and gazing at the horses. The flickering firelight played over their sleek forms. Some had already gone back to grazing. A few had lain down. None appeared concerned about the big cat, which meant they no longer smelled the panther and it must be prowling in another direction.

"Maybe that's it," Tom said. "Maybe there's a real whopper of a panther in these parts, a man-killer. Maybe it's responsible for killing that Crow brave and scaring everyone off."

"The thing is not a panther," Red Moon stated firmly.

"If you say so," Tom said sarcastically. "But if anything shows up, and I don't care if it's one of them Frankenstein monsters or one of those vampyres, I'm going to give it a little surprise." As he finished speaking he reached out and patted his rifle, propped on his saddle beside him.

"There are no such things. All of that is make-believe," Milo said while chewing on a biscuit.

For another 30 minutes they talked. Then the Pennsylvanians and the Crow turned in and Nate started his watch. The Hawken cradled in his left arm, he strolled into the meadow and walked around the horses, Samson sticking with him all the time. The horses were bedded down and quiet.

In the near and far distance arose typical wilderness sounds: the hoots of owls, the howls of wolves, the yips of coyotes, and occasionally the snarls and growls of predators. Stars filled the heavens, a dazzling celestial spectacle that took the breath away.

Nate munched on jerky and took a seat close enough to the fire to be warm, but with his back to it so his night vision wouldn't be impaired by the bright flames. The hours passed uneventfully. When the time came, he awakened Milo and gratefully crawled under his blankets to get some sleep. His last thoughts before drifting to sleep were of the legendary creature. They had been in the valley for hours and it hadn't shown up. Red Moon must be wrong. The Crow was letting the old tales get to him. There was nothing to worry about.

Nothing at all.

Chapter Eleven

The next several days were jammed with activity.

On their second day in the valley they traveled to where the stream forked, debated a bit, and finally decided to go up the right fork first simply because they spied a huge beaver lodge up it, bigger than any of them had ever seen or heard of, and the sight drew them like a magnet. They rode until they could ride no farther, until they found themselves at the base of a steep mountain and saw where the stream came down off that mountain from a high country lake Red Moon said was up near the summit. The water was runoff from the snow that perpetually crowned the surrounding peaks.

Eagerly, they established their first camp. The gear was stripped off the packhorses. All four of them pitched in and constructed a sturdy lean-to that would adequately shelter them from the elements. Their food supply, stored in parfleches and packs, was hung by ropes from high trees limbs to discourage bears and other varmints that might wander by while they were off trapping. Their traps and tools were stored in a corner of the lean-to, but only until the next day, when they began trapping in earnest.

They started out when the sun was still below the horizon, working in pairs. Nate and Red Moon crossed the stream and worked along the west side, exploring up each tributary they discovered. Milo and Tom did likewise on the east side.

Since Red Moon knew little about how to properly set a trap, Nate did most of the work that morning. His traps were all Newhouses, manufactured by Sewell Newhouse of Oneida, New York, from whom they got their nickname. Newhouse sold every type of equipment a trapper needed, and even published a useful manual on the trade that many a beginning trapper carried with him into the vast Rockies.

Laying a trap line was cold, hard work. They hiked from dam to dam. At each, Nate would search for a runway or other likely spot to set his trap. Then he would place the Newhouse flat on the ground, stand on the leaf springs until the jaws dropped open, and adjust the trigger on the disk until the proper tension held the disk in place.

Next the trap was carefully carried into the frigid water and positioned on the bottom so the surface of the water was no more than a hand-width above the disk. This was done because beaver, being short-legged, had to step right on the disk to spring the trap. If the trap was placed any lower, they might swim right over it.

A stout length of wood was then inserted through the ring at the end of the chain and pounded into the bank using the blunt end of a hatchet. Pulling on the chain verified the beaver would be unable to yank it loose.

The last step in setting a trap concerned the bait. Usually contained in small wooden boxes that were frequently sold at the annual rendezvous, the bait consisted of the musky secretion beavers used to mark their territory, and was collected from the glands of dead ones before they were skinned. A thin stick was dipped into the box and then the other end was jabbed into the bank above where the trap had been placed. Once a passing beaver smelled the scent, it would come to investigate, step into the trap, and be caught in rigid steel jaws. Inevitably it drowned, unless the beaver chewed its own foot off to escape, which happened quite often if the traps weren't checked regularly.

Nate took until well past noon to set his 12 traps, and then returned to camp. The two Pennsylvanians had finished much earlier and were already there.

"How did it go?" Tom asked.

"We'll know this evening when we check our lines," Nate replied.

"This evening?" Tom repeated. "But we've always checked our traps in the morning."

"Only once a day?" Nate inquired.

"Sure. What's wrong with that? Many trappers only check their line once a day."

"And they're the ones who lose a lot of beaver. When you only check once a day, it gives any animal you've caught more time to chew its leg off. By checking twice you seldom have one get away on you," Nate said. "Shakespeare himself advised me to check twice and I've always done so."

Milo had been listening attentively. "So that's why we've lost so many. Okay, Nate. From here on out we check twice each day."

"That's a lot of work," Tom grumbled.

"Which would you rather be?" Milo retorted. "Rich or lazy?"

Tom grinned. "Rich, of course. But I hate going into that icy water. It pains my legs something fierce."

"Quite a few trappers have the same complaint," Nate noted. "If you sit by a fire for a while as soon as you're done checking the line, your legs won't hurt half as much."

"I know," Tom said, and shrugged. "You know how it is. We don't always do what is best for us even when we know better."

Red Moon took his bow and quiver from his gear and went off to hunt, leaving his rifle behind. Everyone knew why. Using a gun often spooked game from an area and they wanted to keep the game close so they wouldn't have to spend as much time securing their fresh meat. Over an hour later he came back with a large doe draped over his shoulders.

The sun was close to the western horizon when they went off to check their lines. Nate didn't expect to find many beaver in his traps since the line had been in place for such a short time. To his delight, though, he found three.

At each sprung trap he had to wade into the water and haul the 40-pound carcass onto the bank. After removing the dead animal, he reset the trap in a different spot. Since Red Moon accompanied him, they lugged all three back to camp instead of skinning them on the spot as he would have done had he been alone.

Milo and Tom had not yet returned. Nate placed the three beaver near the fire, obtained his curved skinning knife from his pack, and set to work removing the hides. Many a pelt had been ruined by a man who cut rashly and pierced the soft fur, so he took his time. The better the condition of the pelt, the more money he would make for it.

He had been done for quite some time and darkness was descending when Milo and Tom came back. Five beaver had been snared in their traps and they had removed the hides beside the stream.

Milo glanced at Nate's skins and beamed. "Eight already! I tell you, this venture will pay off handsomely."

Over the next two days his words were borne out. They caught a grand total of 71 beaver, and were kept busy skinning when not checking their lines. They were so busy there was barely time to eat.

By the morning of the fourth day they were all fatigued but elated at their good fortune. Chewing on a flapjack, Milo looked at them and chuckled.

"If we keep going at this rate, we'll have the valley trapped out in a month."

"The sooner, the better," Tom said.

Nate inwardly agreed and was pleased. Between all the beaver along the two upper forks, the dozens of tributaries, and the lower body of the stream, they should each take back between four and five hundred pelts. Not a bad haul at all considering that most trappers took in three or four hundred pelts during an entire year. There were exceptions, of course. Jed Smith had caught close to seven hundred one year. But it was Nate's mentor, Shakespeare McNair, who held the all-time record for a twelve-month haul: 827 pelts.

For three more days they trapped using the same base camp, until the beaver at the head of the fork were almost depleted, and then Nate proposed moving the camp a bit farther down the stream. The move was accomplished in one morning, and by the afternoon they were again working their trap lines.

Red Moon expressed an interest in learning to trap and Nate took it upon himself to teach the old Crow. The warrior's keen mind easily grasped the essentials, and before long Red Moon could trap as well as any of them and skin beaver a lot faster.

On the sixth day in the valley, as evening descended, Nate and Red Moon walked along a narrow creek feeding off the stream, checking their traps. They reached a beaver pond surrounded by high lodgepole pines and worked along the north shore toward a spot where they had placed a Newhouse that morning.

"We caught one," Red Moon said.

A moment later Nate saw the dead beaver submerged in the cold water. He handed his Hawken to the Crow and put his left foot in the pond, idly listening to the nearby chatter of squirrels and the chirping of playful sparrows.

Abruptly, the noises ceased.

Nate had not spent almost five years in the wilderness for nothing. He knew animals never fell silent like that without reason, and the reason invariably was either a roving predator or passing humans. Since there were no other people in the valley except for Benteen and Sublette, who were both over by the fork, the cause for the sudden silence must be a predator.

Visions of a hungry grizzly flitted through Nate's mind and he reached out and took his rifle. The Crow was gazing into the forest, his expression one of questioning curiosity.

Samson uttered a low growl.

Nate looked down at the dog and saw it peering into the wall of vegetation, its nostrils working as it tried to pick up a scent. He cocked the Hawken to be prepared in case there was a grizzly close at hand, then waited for a telltale sign, the crashing of underbrush or the characteristic gruff rumble of a bear in a killing mood.

Time seemed to stand still. The wind had died and not so much as a single leaf fluttered.

As unexpectedly as the interlude began, it ended with the chirp of a robin. The wildlife resumed its normal rhythm of living and the forest was filled with the songs of birds and the buzzing of insects.

"Must have been a bear," Nate speculated.

"No bear," Red Moon said.

"Then what was it?"

"I do not know."

Nate gazed into the Indian's dark eyes, eyes rimmed with wrinkles and reflecting a profound wisdom born of a lifetime spent in the wild. He had the impression Red Moon did know, or had guessed. A possibility occurred to him, but he promptly discarded it. Couldn't be, he told himself. The thing that lurked in the dark only came out at night according to the Indian legends. And besides, there was no such animal.

"I will keep watch while you get the beaver," Red Moon offered.

In half the time it ordinarily required, Nate had the trap out of the water and the beaver out of the trap. His hand fell on his knife, but he paused. If there was a grizzly in the vicinity, perhaps it would be wiser to remove the hide at their camp.

"What about the last trap?" the Crow inquired.

Nate stared off up the creek, remembering the small pond a hundred yards farther on where they had discovered a recently constructed beaver lodge. "I'll go. You take this one back to camp," he proposed.

"We should go together."

"I can manage," Nate insisted. He hefted the Hawken and walked off, Samson beside him as always.

"We should go together," Red Moon insisted, and quickly caught up with them.

Nate glanced at the warrior's impassive features and tried to ascertain the reason the Crow was being so persistent. As if Red Moon knew his thoughts, he met Nate's gaze and spoke softly.

"Perhaps you are right, Grizzly Killer. You have killed many grizzlies, so you must known them well. Perhaps there is a bear out there."

Was Red Moon poking fun at him? Nate wondered, but said nothing. He noticed the Crow had not brought the dead beaver and now held his rifle firmly in both hands.

The last pond in the creek was only 40 feet in circumference, the dam barely five feet high but growing higher every day as the beaver occupying the pond behind it worked continuously at improving the size of their barrier.

Nate walked rapidly, seeing the long shadows all around them and realizing the sun had almost disappeared over the far western horizon, spearing the western sky with vivid streaks of red and orange and pink. The beautiful sunset, which ordinarily would stir his soul mightily, failed to impress him.

The trees were farther back from this pond than the previous one, allowing them to hike around to the opposite side without having to push limbs aside or forge through brush.

Above the surface adjacent to where the stake had been imbedded jutted the rounded tip of a beaver tail.

"Another one," Red Moon said. "We are very fortunate."

"Yes," Nate responded, although secretly he would have been just as happy to find the Newhouse empty. Had it been, they would be on their way to camp. Now he must go into the pond and fetch the carcass.

The frigid mountain water soaked his moccasins and the bottom of his buckskin leggings as he waded in. He grunted when he lifted the beaver, and no wonder, for it was an exceptionally large specimen weighing between 45 and 50 pounds. Once on the bank, he stepped on the leaf springs and yanked the crushed leg out, then stepped aside. The jaws snapped shut with a loud metallic snap.

"We'll skin both at camp," Nate proposed. "I'd like to get back and have a cup of coffee."

"I also," Red Moon said. He pulled the stake out of the ground and dangled the trap from his shoulder by the chain.

As they retraced their steps, Samson between them, Nate mentally chided himself for his nervousness. There was no logical excuse for him to be so jittery. Winona would be ashamed of him if she knew. Not to mention Shakespeare. He squared his shoulders and whistled as they worked their way around the larger pond to where the other trap and beaver lay. But when they got there, he drew up short in surprise.

The trap was exactly where they had left it.

The dead beaver, however, was gone.

Chapter Twelve

"A panther must have taken it," Tom Sublette stated an hour later as they sat around their roaring fire. He squatted beside it, preparing their evening meal.

"That would be my hunch," Milo chimed in.

"I suppose," Nate reluctantly agreed, although deep down he was bothered by an uneasy feeling that a panther had not been responsible. Nor had a grizzly. He couldn't explain the feeling and that worried him even more. There were plenty of tales of mountaineers who inexplicably lost their nerve after two, five, or even ten years in the Rockies and were never the same men again. Day after day, year after year, these men contended with hostile Indians and marauding beasts without batting an eye. Then one day they changed, and they were unable to explain the change to their own or anyone else's satisfaction. But they would pack their belongings and head off for the flatlands never to be seen west of the Mississippi again.

"You don't think so?" Milo asked.

Nate shrugged, unwilling to mention his unfounded anxiety for fear of their ridicule.

"I know!" Tom exclaimed, and laughed. "I'll wager Nate thinks it was the thing that lurks in the dark!"

"I do not," Nate responded, a bit too harshly.

Milo, who had been stretching a hide, stopped and appraised Nate as if he was examining a bug under a microscope. "Did you see any tracks?"

"None," Nate replied. "There was some crushed grass where a heavy foot had pressed, but not a clear print anywhere."

"A heavy foot would mean a bear," Milo mentioned.

"It could have been a bear," Nate said in the hope they would drop the subject. No such luck.

"A bear or a panther, what difference does it make?" Tom stated. "If it has filched a carcass once, it'll be tempted to try taking another. We'll have to be on our guard and keep our rifles handy at all times."

"I intend to do that," Nate said.

Milo devoted his attention to the hide he was working with. "The damnedest thing happened to Tom and me today," he commented offhandedly.

"Oh? What?" Nate asked.

"There we were, walking between traps and talking about the land we want to buy back in Pennsylvania when this is all done with, and all of a sudden the woods became as quiet as a cemetery at midnight. The woods were like a tomb."

Nate exchanged glances with Red Moon.

"Must have been the same critter that stole your beaver," Tom guessed. "It came near us and scared everything within half a mile."

"Must have been," Nate said.

Milo chuckled. "We should count ourselves fortunate the worst we must deal with is a bear or a panther. At least the Blackfeet don't know we're here, or we'd really be in trouble."

Hours later, after Tom and Milo had fallen asleep, Nate lay on his back on his blankets and listened to the horses grazing. Red Moon was on guard and he should have felt safe and comfortable, but he felt neither. Try as he would, he couldn't dispel the odd premonition that all was not well.

A thought struck him with the jolt of a lightning bolt. What if the premonition concerned Winona and Zach? What if they were the ones in danger? He rolled on his side, his forearm under his ear. By now Shakespeare and Blue Water Woman were at the cabin with his wife and son, and there wasn't a man alive who could protect them like McNair.

For that matter, Winona was perfectly capable of looking after herself and their son. She wasn't like many of the refined women Nate had known back in New York City, women who could flash a pretty smile and knew which dress to wear on which occasion and how to dance and curtsy and flutter a fan in the summer heat. A few could cook and fewer could sew, but they all detested the so-called drudgery of maintaining a home. They'd much rather have servants handle such menial work. They didn't seem to realize, as Nate's grandmother had one expressed it, that taking care of a home and rearing a family was the most noble type of work both men and women could hope to perform. And it was only a drudgery if a woman let it be so. His grandmother had often asserted that the three qualities a wife and mother needed most were ingenuity, persistence, and the patience of a rock.

How different Winona was from those pale, spoiled women in New York. She could sew, cook, and butcher an animal with consummate skill. She could hunt, when need be, and she knew scores of edible plants. She knew more about medicinal herbs than any doctor. And, as she had demonstrated time and again, she possessed as much raw courage as any Shoshone warrior.

Lord, she was a woman! He smiled, thinking of the last time they'd clasped one another in a passionate embrace. His lids grew heavy and began to droop, and he was on the verge of falling asleep when the stillness of the night was split by the sound of a branch breaking in half.

Nate sat up, thoroughly awake, and looked in all directions. Some of the horses were feeding, others were lying on the ground. None appeared disturbed. He placed a hand on his rifle, and in doing so brushed his palm against Samson. The dog was gazing to the south but not in the least agitated.

Perhaps it had been Red Moon, Nate decided. He listened for a minute longer, until satisfied there was nothing out there that posed a threat. Then he eased down and closed his eyes. He must stop being so jumpy. By tomorrow his uneasiness would have evaporated like the morning dew and he would feel like a fool for having gotten so worked up over nothing. Despite his assessment, it took him a long, long time to finally drift off.

The next morning he felt remarkably invigorated. As he'd supposed, his anxiety was gone. During the morning hours he diligently checked his traps, retrieved beaver, and repositioned some of the traps where they would do more good. By noon he had ten new pelts to add to their swiftly accumulating haul. That night, eight more.

One busy day after another went by. A week elapsed. Two. Two and a half. They worked their way down the right fork and camped at the junction.

"Tomorrow," Milo said in anticipation as they sat around the fire shortly after sunrise, "we start up the left fork. And if there are half as many beaver as there were up the right fork, we'll be rolling in prime furs."

Nate nodded and sipped at his steaming coffee. Their camp lay in a clearing nestled among the pines where they were sheltered from the often chilly night winds. Northwest of them, picketed in a field, were the horses.

"We should have toted more traps in," Tom remarked.

"A man can only do so much, can only check so many traps in a single day," Nate said. "We have all we'll need."

Red Moon, who sat with a blanket draped over his shoulders, suddenly straightened, letting the blanket fall, and pivoted in the direction of the valley entrance. "Listen," he said.

Nate did, and heard nothing out of the ordinary. "What is it?"

"Someone comes. One man on horseback."

Tom stood. "The hell you say. I don't hear a thing."

"Grab your guns and take cover," Nate directed, scooping up the Hawken. He ran to the trees bordering the stream and leaned his shoulder against a tree trunk. From where he stood he had a clear view of the stream for hundreds of yards.

A second later a lone rider appeared, proceeding up the east bank.

Nate studied the man, immediately seeing it was an Indian. From the way the warrior wore his hair, swept back on either side with a large eagle feather attached to the top of his head, and from the style of his long buckskin shirt and leggings, Nate recognized the tribe the man belonged to. His stomach muscles involuntarily tightened.

He was a Blackfoot.

The brave carried a lance in his right hand and had a bow and quiver slanted across his back. He was leaning low, concentrating on the ground.

Nate glanced at Milo and Tom, hidden nearby, and saw the anxiety on their faces. With good reason. That Blackfoot was following the trail they had made when they first entered the valley weeks ago. It had only rained once, briefly, in all that time, so the hoofprints of their horses were undoubtedly still evident.

Nate shifted and glanced to his left, where Red Moon stood behind a pine tree. The Crow, as always, did not betray his feelings. But he had his rifle cocked.

The Blackfoot reined up two hundred yards off and surveyed the valley. Then he swung down, dropped to one knee, and ran his hand over the tracks.

Nate could imagine what the brave was thinking. The Blackfoot would know that white men were in the party because the horses ridden by Benteen and Sublette were shod, as were their pack animals. Nate had long since stopped bothering to shoe his horses, preferring to ride them unshod as did the Indians.

From the heavier tracks of the pack animals, the Blackfoot would be able to deduce exactly how many men were with the group. He would probably suspect there were two Indians and two whites, and he would be greatly perplexed. What was such a mixed group doing in this valley so close to Blackfoot territory? Since the Crows occupied the region to the south, he might suspect there to be a Crow encampment somewhere farther up the stream.

Nate watched, debating whether to shoot. He refrained because he doubted very much the brave was alone. The warrior might be part of a war party heading into Crow land, and if so, the rest of the band might hear any shot and come to investigate. Had he been closer he would have tried to get the man with his knife. Under the circumstances, there was nothing he could do.

At length the Blackfoot rose and scanned the forest. Gripping his mount's mane, he vaulted onto the animal and yanked sharply on the rope reins. Using his feet and his quirt, he urged the white horse into a gallop and raced back the way he had come.

"Damn!" Milo fumed.

"He'll be back with his friends," Tom snapped. "Now we're in for it."

Nate led them to their camp. The Pennsylvanians were sullen and silent. Red Moon moved to one side and folded his arms across his chest.

"Well, I'll tell you now," Tom declared. "I'm not about to pack up and run off with my tail tucked between my legs because of the rotten Blackfeet. This valley is a gold mine in furs, and I'm not giving up my chance to go home with my pockets filled with money."

"I agree," Milo said. "We've worked too hard to call it quits at this stage. I say we stick it out."

Nate swung toward the Crow. "And you?"

Red Crow grinned. "I like to kill Blackfeet."

"Then it's settled," Nate said. "We stay and keep trapping."

"You haven't told us how you feel," Milo noted.

"I'm not too keen on tangling with the Blackfeet," Nate answered. "But I'm like you. I want to get as many peltries as I can before we leave."

"Good," Tom said, and wagged his rifle. "If those devils show their faces, we'll make their squaws widows."

"There's bound to be a shooting scrape," Milo commented, and frowned.

"From now on we must do things differently," Nate told them. "We can't leave our camp unattended at any time. So we'll take turns in the morning and evening checking our trap lines. One day Red Moon and I can go out first and then the two of you can go after we get back, and the next day we'll switch and you two can check your line first. Sound fair?"

"Sounds perfect," Milo said.

"We must also select our campsites with more care," Nate recommended. "We can't camp in the open and we must always build our fires under trees so the smoke will thin out as it rises."

"And never use our guns," Red Moon said.

Nate looked at him. "Since you're the best with a bow and arrow, you'll have to do the hunting from now on."

"I will," Red Moon said, and walked across the clearing toward the horses.

"Where are you going?" Tom asked.

"I will find out how many Blackfeet there are," Red Moon replied. "Do not expect me back before dark."

"Be careful," Nate cautioned.

"Always."

They watched the Crow mount his horse and ride off bareback, his long hair flying, man and horse one.

"I'm glad he's with us," Milo said.

Nate gripped the Hawken in his left hand. "Since I doubt the Blackfeet will be paying us a visit in the next hour or so, I'll go on up the left fork and see if there are as many beaver there as we've found elsewhere."

"Alone?" Milo said.

"I'll have Samson," Nate reminded him, and started off, the dog so close to his leg he had to be careful not to accidentally bump into it. He stuck to the inner bank and came on a large pond with a huge lodge within minutes. The vegetation pressed right up to the water's edge and he had to fight his way through to the high dam. Beyond lay another pond, another lodge.

Onward he went. As with the other fork and the lower branch, beaver sign was everywhere. He also saw the tracks of deer, elk, and smaller critters in the mud along the stream. Raccoons, skunks, bobcats, and more all came regularly to drink, and he was able to determine when they had done so and their approximate size and weight from the impressions they'd left.

Four more lodges he discovered, and then he paused beside another dam and absently gazed at the bare earth near its base. For several seconds he stared at a peculiar depression, thinking it must have been made when a large rock was dislodged. But there were no rocks anywhere near the dam, and suddenly he realized what the depression really was. His breath caught in his throat and his eyes widened in amazement.

It was a huge footprint.

Chapter Thirteen

Nate dashed down the slope toward the base of the dam and slipped on the slick ground. His left leg flew out from under him and he wildly flapped his arms to retain his balance. He reached the base upright, halted abruptly, and slowly sank into a crouch so he could study the marvel before him.

The track was unlike any he'd ever seen. Roughly square in shape, the heel being only slightly tapered, it measured approximately 15 inches in length and seven inches in width at the ball of the foot. Unlike bear tracks, which invariably gave some evidence of the bear's nonretractable claws, this one displayed the distinct impressions of five large toes, toes very humanlike in shape and arrangement.

Awed by the dimensions, Nate whispered in awe, "What in heaven's name is this?" He placed his right hand in the center of the track and saw how the track dwarfed it. Then he stood and placed his foot beside the track; his foot seemed like that of a small child's in comparison.

He cast around for more tracks but found none. Mystified, he walked back to the print and then noticed his own tracks. Where he'd walked in the mud, his moccasins sank to a depth of less than a quarter of an inch. But the huge print, by contrast, was a good inch and a half deep, which meant whatever made it had been extremely heavy.

Nate stood over the strange print and pondered. He thought of every animal that inhabited the Rockies and their tracks. None came close to resembling this one, not even the tracks of grizzlies. Either the impression had been produced by natural circumstances, by a means he could not fathom, or a totally unknown animal had made it.

The thing that lurked in the dark!

Unbidden, the Crow legend sprang to mind. He glanced up and scanned the surrounding forest, but saw nothing out of the ordinary. Birds were singing in carefree abandon. Had there been anything unusual in the area they would fall silent.

He walked in a circle around the track, inspecting it from every angle, mulling his course of action. If he went back and told the Pennsylvanians, they would be skeptical. Even if he showed it to them, they might not be willing to believe the creature behind the Crow legend had been responsible for making it. Considering how badly they wanted to acquire stakes so they could buy land in Pennsylvania, they certainly wouldn't be willing to leave the valley simply because a peculiar track had been found.

Nate halted and scratched his chin. If he was right, and the creature had made it, then what did it mean? Had the creature bothered them in any way since they entered the valley? No. Had they seen hide or hair of it? No. Had their trapping been affected? No.

Suddenly he recalled the missing dead beaver. What if the creature had taken it? Had it been watching them? Had it seen him pull the beaver out of the pond and then go off, leaving it unattended? Had it been hungry and decided to venture from concealment and grab the tempting meal? He had no way of knowing for certain, but the supposition made sense.

It also troubled him. If the creature did exist, and if it had stolen the beaver, then it meant the creature ate meat. It was carnivorous, a predator like a panther or a lynx. Or maybe it was more like a grizzly, which would eat practically anything under the sun. Grizzlies not only ate anything they could catch, including small and large animals, but they would also eat certain roots, sprouts, berries, and insects. Not to mention their fondness for fish. And grizzlies would kill and eat a man just as readily as they would a trout.

Did this creature have similar eating habits? If so, why hadn't it attacked any of them yet? Was it afraid of them, the Crow tales notwithstanding? Or was it because they nearly always worked in pairs?

He shook his head and sighed. There were too few facts to go on and his suppositions were meaningless. He held the Hawken in his left hand, trying to decide whether to go back to camp and inform Benteen and Sublette or continue scouting the fork. His eyes fell on Samson, who was lying a few yards away. The dog's eyes were on him. They seldom left him nowadays, and he knew Samson had developed quite an attachment to him.

An idea occurred to him. What if the creature was shying away from them because of Samson? Large animals such as grizzlies and panthers were naturally wary of one another, and this might be the same case.

On second thought, Nate discarded the notion. The thing that had made the huge footprint must be incredibly big and extraordinarily powerful. Such a brute would have no reason to fear a dog, or humans for that matter.

"Samson," he said softly, and Samson lifted his head. "Come here, boy."

The black dog rose and padded over.

"Here," Nate said, touching the track. "What do you think?"

Samson lowered his head and touched Nate's hand with his nose. Then he stiffened and sniffed loudly, not once but several times, while moving his head around the edge of the track. Stepping back, he vented a short growl.

"I feel the same way," Nate said. Facing up the stream, he resumed walking. He wanted to go farther, to check for more beaver. If, along the way, he happened to find another such track, so much the better.

For the better part of an hour he hiked, finding a series of lodges and dams just like on the other fork. Once he saw a large beaver swimming out near a lodge, but the beaver paid no notice to him. Twice he saw elk back in the brush.

He found no more huge tracks, which disappointed him. The single impression had been insufficient to tell him much about the creature. He could guess at its size and weight, but he would have a better idea of both if he could find a set of tracks and determine the length of its stride. Competent trackers, by taking account of the distance between two tracks, could accurately gauge the height of the animal or person making them.

He would also have liked to trail the beast to its lair. If he could get to it before it got to them, he could judge for himself whether the thing deserved to be shot or whether it was actually a harmless animal. Given that they had been in the valley for weeks without being bothered, he inclined to the opinion the Crow stories were greatly exaggerated.

At last he turned back and retraced his route to the camp. Halfway back he stopped, bothered by a vague feeling of being watched. He scoured the undergrowth but saw no reason for the feeling. Since Samson was not acting as if something might be out there, he ascribed his jitters to another case of bad nerves and continued on.

"How does it look?" Milo asked as soon as Nate appeared.

"There are as many beaver up the left fork as there were up the right, if not more."

Tom, who was near the rekindled fire and busy repairing a small hole in his left moccasin, nodded and beamed. "I can almost feel that money in my pocket. Red Moon has done us a big favor by bringing us here."

"Maybe we should pay him a little extra," Milo suggested.

"Are you crazy?" Tom rejoined. "He's earning enough to keep him in whiskey for the rest of his life. Ten percent is plenty. A bit too much, in my estimation."

"Ten percent is what we agreed on and ten percent is what we'll give him," Milo said.

Nate was tempted to tell them the reason Red Moon wanted the money, until it hit him that the Crow might not care for them to know. Red Moon had been with Milo and Tom for many weeks before they showed up at the cabin, and in all that time the warrior had not bothered to let them know about his ailing grandson. Why Red Moon had told him instead of them, he didn't know. But he wasn't about to violate the Crow's confidence. If Red Moon elected to tell them, that was his business.

"You're too soft, Milo," Tom was saying. "He's just an Injun. What does he know about money?"

Resentful of the disparaging comments about Red

Moon, Nate elected to change the topic of conversation and did so by announcing, "I saw a strange track."

They stared at him, both puzzled by the declaration.

"A what?" Tom said.

"A track bigger than any I've ever come across," Nate elaborated.

"Do you mean a bear print?" Milo asked.

"No. There was no sign of claws. I have no idea what made it. I'd like to show it to you so you can see for yourselves and give me your opinion."

Tom snickered. "Perhaps it was the thing Red Moon is so scared of."

"Perhaps," Nate said.

"You're joking, King," Tom stated.

"No, I'm not."

"Where did you find this—" Milo began, then fell silent when the drumming of hoofs sounded from the south.

Instantly on his feet, Nate spied Red Moon galloping toward their camp. The Crow was using his quirt as if trying to ride his horse into the ground.

"Trouble," Milo said, clutching his rifle.

"Damn it all," Tom muttered, hastily slipping his left foot into his moccasin even though he hadn't completed the repair.

Nate advanced to the edge of the clearing. He gazed past the Crow, seeking any sign of pursuing Blackfeet, but there was none. The Crow arrived with a clatter of hoofs and jerked hard on the reins.

"A Blackfoot war party is coming."

"How many and how far off are they?" Nate inquired, suppressing a swell of anxiety. Rare was the trapping party that didn't run into some sort of grave difficulty. They'd been exceptionally lucky so far and hadn't lost a single man or animal. All that might be about to change.

"There are ten warriors, all well armed," Red Moon

disclosed, and slid to the grass. "I saw them when I climbed a tree to see how close I was to the man I followed. From a high branch I saw him riding toward a group waiting down the stream."

Nate didn't need to be told the rest. That lone brave, who had been sent on ahead to scout the trail, would rejoin the other Blackfeet and the whole group would head on up the valley with dreams of counting coup on white men foremost in their heads. And once the war party reached the spot where Red Moon had turned around and ridden back they would know the brave had been seen and the white men were forewarned. They would press on swiftly, eager to take scalps.

"I say we make a stand right here," Tom declared.

Nate studied the lay of the land. They were ringed by trees, but there was plenty of cover for the Blackfeet to creep right up on them before they knew it. And they would be unable to adequately protect the horses. "They'd overrun us in no time," he said.

"What do we do?" Milo asked.

In his mind's eye Nate reviewed the course of the right fork and remembered a point where the stream curved to the northeast. There were large boulders flanking the east bank, not many but enough to hide behind and ambush the Blackfeet when they showed up. He voiced his idea.

"Sounds fine to me," Milo said, and stooped to pick up his saddle and blanket.

"That spot is half a day's ride away," Tom groused. "Isn't there somewhere nearer?"

"None that are any better," Nate said, "and we'll need the most defensible position we can find if we're to hold off ten Blackfeet."

In silence they worked, rapidly loading their traps, food, and gear onto the pack animals and saddling their horses. When they were all mounted, Nate took the lead and cantered along the bank. Samson padded on his right.

"Nate, you've done more Indian fighting than we have," Milo said. "What are our chances against this bunch? Realistically, I mean."

"Not very good."

"If they gain the upper hand and it looks as if we'll be taken prisoner, promise me you'll put a ball in my brain before they get their hands on us."

Nate shifted to glance at the lean Pennsylvania.

"I've heard about the tortures those red devils inflict," Milo said. "They stake a man out and do all sorts of hideous acts. They poke out eyeballs, cut off noses, and slice off tongues. They've been known to rip a man's guts out while he's still alive. And I heard about that Frenchman they skinned alive." He shuddered. "I don't want any of that to happen to me. I couldn't take it."

"I promise," Nate said.

"Those heathens won't get us if I can help it," Tom asserted. "I'll fight until I drop, and I'll take as many of their black souls with me as I can."

The sun climbed steadily higher. They slowed every now and then, saving their mounts in case a burst of speed should be needed. Several times Red Moon left them and rode back to see if the Blackfeet were gaining. Each time he caught up again and informed them the trail was clear.

Except for taking brief breaks to allow the horses to drink, they didn't stop. By late afternoon the boulders came into view.

"We made it," Milo said in relief.

Beyond the boulders was a field where they tied the horses, leaving both their saddles and the packs on for the time being. Nate took his rifle and took up a post behind the boulder nearest the stream. Samson reclined nearby and dozed, unaffected by their tension.

"Now all we can do is wait," Milo remarked.

Nate leaned on his left shoulder, tucked the Hawken in the crook of his arm, and settled down for a possibly long wait. The Blackfeet were experienced, canny fighters, and once they believed they were close to overhauling their intended victims they would slow down and proceed cautiously. He didn't expect them until near dark.

Warmed by the sun and feeling a bit fatigued after the long ride, Nate gazed at the stream and considered taking a drink. He forgot about his thirst the next moment, however, when he saw something that prickled the short hairs at the nape of his neck.

Another enormous track.

Chapter Fourteen

Projecting into the stream from the bank was a finger of land around which the water flowed at a slow rate. On that narrow strip was the footprint, the same size as the one found on the left fork, the toes pointing downstream.

Nate was tempted to run out for a closer look, but the Blackfeet might show up at any minute. A disturbing insight struck him. What if the creature had been shadowing them? What if that track had been made as the thing trailed them toward the junction? The only way he could know for sure was to closely examine the track later.

The gurgling water provoked another train of thought. Both tracks he'd discovered were located near water. Was it possible the creature preferred to travel along the streams and creeks so it wouldn't leave many clues of its passing? Trappers, when chased by Indians, often resorted to riding along a watercourse in an attempt to lose pursuers. But he'd never heard of an animal adopting a similar practice.

He glanced at the others. Milo was staring intently to the south. Tom was sharpening his butcher knife. Red Moon was staring at the track. The Crow looked at him and neither of them spoke. There was no need. They both knew what had made it—at least they knew the creature existed and was aware of their presence in the valley. At the moment, however, it was the least of their worries.

Slowly the glowing sun sank toward the western horizon. The shadows lengthened and the depths of the forest became dark and foreboding.

"Where the hell are they?" Tom muttered.

"Are you in a hurry to be killed?" Milo whispered.

"No, but if we're going to be in a shooting scrape I'd rather get it over with now than wait," Tom responded.

Nate shared those sentiments. As the minutes crawled past with all the speed of sluggish earthworms, he became increasingly restless. It was apparent the Blackfeet had no intention of launching their attack before dawn since they rarely if ever fought at night. When the sun had dipped so low that only a rosy rim remained, he straightened. "They plan to try for our hair tomorrow," he stated.

"Why are they waiting?" Milo asked.

"Why should they rush things and lose more men than they have to?" Nate rejoined. "There's only one way out of this valley, and they must know it. They have us boxed in." He moved toward their horses, Samson walking in his footsteps. "No, they'll rest up tonight and tackle us tomorrow, probably after they spy on us a while. They'll pick the time for our fight, and there's not a blessed thing we can do about it."

"Grizzly Killer is correct," Red Moon said. "The Blackfeet will attack when they are ready and not before." He paused. "Maybe they have sent someone for more warriors."

Nate hadn't considered that angle. It worried him profoundly. If there were more Blackfeet in the general area, and if another ten or more joined the first bunch, the likelihood of escaping from the valley was almost non-existent.

"Do we stay put or move elsewhere?" Milo inquired.

The encroaching veil of night allowed only one answer. "We stay right where we are," Nate said. "It would be useless to go traipsing around in the dark searching for a better spot."

Milo nodded in agreemnt. "Can we have a fire?"

"A small one, if you build it behind the boulders where the glow can't be seen and keep it small so there isn't much smoke," Nate instructed him.

For the next half an hour they were busy tending to their stock. The horses were watered and picketed to graze. Since they weren't anticipating an attack, the packs and saddles were removed. Milo got a fire going and made a pot of coffee and cooked venison steaks carved from a buck Red Moon had shot with an arrow the day before.

None of them were talkative. Each ate quietly, immersed in his thoughts. Every so often Tom Sublette would turn to the south and glare into the darkness, his thoughts transparent.

Nate dwelled on their predicament and tried to devise a way out. Trying to sneak past the Blackfeet at night would be impossible since they were bound to post braves at various points across the valley floor until morning. He weighed the merits of sneaking down to the Blackfoot camp and shooting as many as possible, finally deciding the risks were greater than any prospect of reducing the odds.

When the meal was over, Milo took the utensils

down to the stream to wash them. Tom went along as escort.

No sooner were they out of hearing range than Red Moon swiveled to face Nate. "None of us may leave this place alive."

"I know."

"The Blackfeet will find us. Then they will surround us and close in on us when our guard is down."

"I know."

"I am a warrior, Grizzly Killer. I have counted twenty-seven coup in my life. I have fought the Blackfeet, the Bloods, the Utes, and the Cheyennes. I have killed men with my knife, my tomahawk, my bow, and my rifle. It is not in me to sit by and let my enemies pick the time and place for me to die."

Nate lowered his coffee cup. "What do you propose?"

"Before the sun rises we must be awake and have our horses ready to ride. Then we must sneak down the valley, past the Blackfoot camp, and head for the valley entrance," Red Moon proposed.

"They'll probably spot us."

"Would you rather sit here and wait to die?"

"No," Nate admitted. "I like your plan." He leaned against the boulder and let the fire warm his feet. Although once he would have scoffed at the notion, he was a fighter. Repeatedly he'd been thrust into life-threatening situations where he either had to resist or die, and each time he'd chosen to struggle with all his might to live. Yes, he was a fighter, and it galled him to contemplate defeat. He had a wife and a son who loved him. He fully intended to see them again, and he would fight tooth and claw to preserve his life.

The two Pennsylvanians returned. Nate outlined the ploy they would use, then offered to take the first watch while the others slept. They spread out their blankets at the edge of the firelight so they wouldn't be easy targets should a Blackfoot creep up on them, leaving Nate alone at the boulder.

He tried not to dwell on the war party. Instead, he mused on the whims of circumstance that often dictated the course of a person's life. A man or woman never knew from one day to the next what subsequent days would bring, and each was at the mercy of a capricious fate that held no regard for anyone. How many trappers had he known, good men who worked hard, who were honest to a fault, but who had perished at the hands of marauding Indians? How many decent trappers had lost their lives through a freakish accident, never to see their kin back in the States again? What had those men done to deserve deaths? Nothing. And yet they went to meet their Maker ahead of their allotted time.

A month ago he had been comfortable and safe in his cabin. Now he was on the verge of battling bloodthirsty Blackfeet and might well lose his life. And all because of a series of circumstances over which he had no control. Had the Pennsylvanians never gotten it into their heads to enlist his help, he would still be comfortable and safe in his cabin.

Still, the decision to come with them had been his. When a man got right down to the bone of the matter, decisions determined a man's fate more than circumstances. Decisions were reactions to circumstances, and it was those reactions that determined whether a man lived or died, grew rich or poor, lived happily or miserably.

Lost in reflection, he didn't realize how much time elapsed until with a start he saw the fire had burned down to glowing embers. He rose and gathered more wood, then fed the embers until a crackling fire again brightened the night. Walking to Milo, he shook the lean trapper.

"What?" Milo mumbled, his eyelids fluttering.

"You agreed to take the second watch," Nate said. "Spell me."

"Oh. Yes," Milo said sleepily. Rousing himself, he pushed to his feet, wiped his eyes with the back of his hands, and took his rifle over to where Nate had sat. "Anything?"

"Nothing. Keep your eyes skinned."

"You don't need to tell me twice," Milo replied, and stretched.

Nate spread out his bedroll and lay on his back, the Hawken at his side. Samson claimed the left side of the blanket, his back pressed flush against Nate.

"Did you see this fire?" Milo asked.

"What's wrong with it? I just gathered more dead branches," Nate answered.

"No, not *our* fire. This other fire."

Milo was standing out past the boulder when Nate joined him. In the far distance to the south, flickering faintly, was another camp fire.

"The Blackfeet," Milo deduced.

"Yep."

"How far do you reckon they are?"

"It's hard to judge at night," Nate said.

"I'm surprised they'd let us know where they are," Milo said.

"They're not afraid of us. The Blackfeet are the most murderous lot of Indians this side of the divide, but there is no denying their courage. They don't care if we know where they are. If we should attack them, so much the better. They won't need to come looking for us."

Milo cocked an eye. "You give me the impression you admire these savages."

"I admire courage in any man, Indian or white," Nate responded, and rotated. He took a stride when his ears caught a fluttering sound, so indistinct as to make him believe he had imagined hearing it. Pausing, he turned and listened.

"What is it?" Milo inquired.

"I don't know," Nate said, and then he heard a slightly louder sound, a long, high-pitched, wavering cry.

"Dear Lord!" Milo exclaimed. "What in the world was that?"

From behind them came the clipped voice of Red Moon. "A scream," he said, walking forward.

"The Blackfeet must have captured someone else," Milo speculated. "Perhaps another trapper."

The wind, which had been wafting from north to south, chose that instant to die completely and the air hung still as death around them. Without the wind to stir the trees and grass, an eerie silence ensued. In that silence, from the direction of the speck of light to the south, there came a hair-raising series of terrified screams and screeches attended by the boom of gunfire. Once, as clear as a church bell on a Sunday morning, a horse whinnied as if in abject fright.

"What's happening over there?" Milo breathed.

The frantic screams and screeches rent the night interminably. Their own horses neighed and stamped in nervous agitation.

Milo cast a bewildered gaze at Nate. "It's like they're in a war or something."

"Or something."

"Now it begins," Red Moon declared solemnly.

"What begins?" Milo asked.

The Crow didn't answer.

Every time Nate heard one of those horrifying cries, a twinge rippled along his spine. His skin crawled as if of its own volition. There could only be one explanation in his estimation, and the knowledge created an icy chill in the depths of his soul.

"What the hell is happening?" Tom Sublette demanded as he stepped past the boulder. "Why are the horses—"

"Shhhhh," Milo hissed. "Listen!"

The distant din went on for another minute or two before diminishing in volume and tapering off on a single plaintive note of raw despair.

"What *was* that?" Tom inquired.

"The Blackfeet," Nate said. He moved to the fire and squatted on his heels to pour coffee into his tin cup.

"I don't understand," Milo said. "Why would the Blackfeet be carrying on that way?"

"It was a trick," Tom stated. "They want us to ride to their camp to investigate so they can spring an ambush on us."

"You didn't hear as much as we did," Milo disputed him. "It was no trick. Those devils were fighting for their lives."

"Against who?" Tom demanded.

Nate let some of the warm coffee trickle into his mouth and swished the brew with his tongue before swallowing. "We must go find out."

"Are you touched in the head? It's a trap, I tell you," Tom insisted. "Go there and some buck will be showing your hair to his sweetheart when he gets back to his village."

Red Moon knelt and commenced folding his blanket. "We must go."

"You too?" Tom responded. "What's gotten into the two of you? At least wait until morning when we can see."

"Now," Nate said, and swallowed once more. He spilled the rest of the coffee on the grass and stood.

Milo frowned and stepped closer. "What is it? What do Red Moon and you know that we don't? What will we find down there?"

"I don't know," Nate said. But he did. He knew,

deep within the well of his being. He knew, and he cursed himself for being the biggest fool who'd ever lived.

Tom made an angry gesture. "Will someone please tell me what the hell is going on? Since when do we go riding around in the middle of the night?"

"If you don't want to tag along you're welcome to stay here by yourself," Nate told him.

Glancing to the south, Tom took less than five seconds to reach a decision. "No thanks. Where you gents go, I go. I just hope you know what the hell you're doing."

So do I, Nate thought. So do I.

Chapter Fifteen

A crimson hue tinged the eastern horizon when Nate drew rein and tilted his head to sniff the air. He smelled the lingering scent of wood smoke and something else, a revolting stench that nearly made him gag. Hundreds of feet away, rising sluggishly on the slight air currents, was a thin column of gray smoke.

"The Blackfoot camp," Milo said softly.

Nate nodded and attached the lead rope to his packhorses to a low branch. The Crow was already moving to the right to approach the site from a different angle. He looked at the Pennsylvanians and pointed to their left.

Tom promptly tied his pack animals to a tree limb and waited for Milo to do likewise, and together they started circling.

The feel of the invariably reliable Hawken in Nate's left hand, which usually inspired him with confidence when he confronted danger, failed to assuage his growing uneasiness. Placing the rifle across his thighs, he glanced down at Samson and rode onward. The nauseating smell grew stronger and stronger with each stride his stallion took, forcing him to breathe shallowly to keep his stomach from tossing.

He was within 25 yards of the wispy tendril of smoke when the stallion suddenly shied from an object lying directly in their path, an object he'd assumed to be a broken limb. Stopping, he bent forward and involuntarily gasped.

The limb wasn't from any tree. Lying in the shadow of a pine, the skin bronzed from constant exposure to the sun, was a human arm. The fingers were locked like claws. Ribbons of severed flesh dangled from the top of the upper arm where it had been violently torn from the shoulder.

Nate skirted the grisly legacy of the nocturnal battle and made for the smoke. He hadn't gone another five yards when he came on the body to which the arm had once belonged.

The Blackfoot lay on his back, his lifeless eyes fixed blankly on the canopy of limbs above him. A puddle of blood had seeped into the ground from his ravaged shoulder. Torn leggings covered his legs.

Nate stared at the man's face and scowled. The Blackfoot wore an expression of stark terror, his features contorted in a grotesque mockery of a human visage. What had the warrior seen in those last moments of life that provoked such terror?

He prodded the stallion with his heels. Soon a clearing opened up before him. All that remained of the fire were flickering coals and the ascending smoke. Littering the area around that fire in all directions, sprawled in postures of gruesome death, were more Blackfeet.

Nate stopped at the edge of the trees and tucked the stock of the Hawken against his side, his thumb on

the hammer. He surveyed the clearing and bile rose
in his throat. With an effort, he swallowed it. Never
had he seen such carnage. Never would he care to view
such unspeakable slaughter again.

The clearing might aptly be termed a battlefield.
That a tremendous fight had occurred was evidenced
by the many dead and the many pools of drying blood,
by the arrows and lances and guns scattered about,
and by the torn parfleches, the ripped blankets, and the
occasional articles of scattered clothing.

There were 17 Blackfoot warriors in all, young and
old alike, most splotched with bloodstains. Quite a
few had dried blood ringing their parted lips. Every
one bore evidence of having received a vicious beating.
Bruises marred their faces and torsos. There were bite
marks on nearly each brave, and over half showed
several spots where their flesh had been ripped from
their bodies. Many had broken arms or legs, as displayed by the unnatural angles at which the limbs
were extended. One warrior was on his stomach but
his head had been twisted completely around so that
his wide-eyed gaze was fixed on his heels.

Nate heard retching and glanced to his left. Milo
was hunched over a bush, his back to the clearing.
Sublette, still on horseback, seemed pale. Nate swung
to the right and saw Red Moon walking among the
fallen. Easing from the saddle, he stepped into the
open.

A husky brave nearby had been gutted, his abdomen
ruptured. A pile of pale, pulpy intestines rested on the
crushed grass beside him. Another warrior had a
caved-in chest. His ribs and sternum curved sharply
inward and jagged tips of busted rib bones poked from
his taut skin. A third brave had lost half of his forehead
and his left cheek.

A fly flew close to Nate's face and he swatted it aside.
It recovered in midair and flew to a corpse, where it

settled on the warrior's smashed nose. There were more flies on the same man, and gazing over the clearing Nate spotted scores if not hundreds of flies flitting about on the bodies.

"Who could have done this?" Tom Sublette asked.

"Who?" Nate said.

"Which tribe? The Utes don't range this far north, or so I've been told," Tom mentioned. "Could it have been the Crows?"

Red Moon heard the query. "My people did not do this."

"Then who? Are there tribes to the west I don't know about who can lick the Blackfeet so handily?" Tom inquired.

"This was not done by men," Red Moon informed him.

Sublette halted, blinked, and grinned. "You're not going to try and convince me that the goblin who supposedly lives in this valley was responsible, are you?"

"See for yourself," Nate said, halting near the fire where there was bare earth. Next to the shattered leg of a Blackfoot was the outline of a by-now-familiar track.

"See what?" Tom said, and walked over. Consternation lined his countenance and he squatted. "This can't be what it looks like."

"It's the same sort of track I saw up the left fork," Nate stated.

"There must be a logical explanation for it," Tom said, his tone lacking much conviction. "Maybe it's a bear print."

"Then where are the claw marks?"

"I don't know. Maybe it lost its claws in an accident."

"You know better."

The stocky Pennsylvania touched the track, then

stood. His eyes were troubled when he faced Nate. "The creature did all of this?" he asked, sweeping the clearing with an emphatic wave of his arm.

Red Moon walked toward them, and for the first time his emotions were plain for anyone to read. He was profoundly upset, as his strained tone confirmed. "Yes," he answered Sublette. "There are not many tracks of the thing that lurks in the dark, but the sign is clear enough to know what happened."

"Tell us," Tom urged.

The Crow nodded at the west side of the clearing, the side nearest the stream. "It came up out of the water and stood for a long time watching the Blackfeet. They did not know it was there. Knowing them as I do, I would say they were busy getting ready for their attack on us. They must have talked until late about their plan. Then, when their weapons were all in order, most of them went to sleep. They would have wanted to be rested when morning came."

"And then?" Tom said when the Crow paused.

Red Moon scanned the ground, pointing at specific points as he talked. "The beast made some noise to draw the guard into the forest. His tracks lead off that way," he said, indicating due north.

"I found him," Nate revealed. "His arm had been torn from its socket."

"With the guard dead, the thing was free to do as it wanted," Red Moon said. He motioned at four Blackfeet lying in a row, each with his throat crushed. "It came into the camp and killed those four before the Blackfeet knew what was happening. Another must have woken up, seen it, and shouted the alarm."

Nate scoured the vegetation, wondering if the thing was still lurking nearby or whether it had gone off to its lair, wherever that might be.

"The rest were awake in no time and fighting for their lives," Red Moon continued as Milo shuffled up to them. "They fought bravely but they were confused and very, very scared."

"What do you mean by they were confused?" Tom inquired, hanging on every word the aged warrior spoke.

Red Moon walked to a corpse and flicked his right foot out to touch an arrow jutting from the Blackfoot's chest. "This one was shot by another member of the war party," he said, and swiveled. "There are more, warriors who were slain by arrows or lances or were shot by a gun."

Nate looked and saw several examples. He'd missed it before because he'd been concentrating on finding evidence of the creature. But Red Moon was right. The scene must have been sheer chaos. Mental images of the frightened Blackfeet fighting valiantly for their lives in the frantic jumble of whirling companions made him see how easily the accidents must have happened.

"The horses ran off, leaving the men on foot," Red Moon detailed as he moved in a circle, his alert eyes missing none of the sign underfoot. "A few ran. The rest stayed. They would not desert their friends."

"But there were twenty or more Blackfeet and only one creature," Tom said in exasperation. "How could one animal lick them?"

Red Moon nodded at a brave whose head had been split open, exposing the brain. "The beast must have knocked many down, breaking their bones or cracking their heads, and then gone around later and finished them off."

"But they must have hit it!" Tom asserted. "They couldn't all miss! Why didn't it die?"

"I do not know," Red Moon said. "But I do know it went from man to man, killing them in its own sweet time. Look there." He pointed at a Blackfoot whose neck and face had been gnawed down to the bone. "It ate parts of them."

"Oh, God," Milo said. "Oh, God."

Tom kicked at the dying fire. "Damn it all! There's no way one animal could have killed so many Blackfeet and gotten off without a scratch. The thing must be lying in the brush, about dead from its wounds."

"Perhaps," Red Moon said.

Milo pressed a hand to his stomach, his mouth curling downward. "You say a few got away?"

"Three. They ran toward the valley entrance."

"Maybe they will come back with others," Milo said.

"No. They have learned their lesson. The only reason they entered the valley was to take our scalps, and now they will never enter again," Red Moon stated.

Milo gave each of them a quizzical glance. "What do we do? Stay or leave?"

"How can you even ask?" Tom rejoined. "We can't give up now, not when there are so many beaver left."

"I don't much care about the beaver anymore," Milo said.

"And I suppose you don't care about the stakes we've been counting on to buy the land we want?" Tom snapped. "If we leave now, we may never raise the money to have our own farms."

With an air of haunted indecision, Milo regarded the bloody carnage. "Is it worth risking our lives for?"

Nate rested the stock of his Hawken between his feet and lightly gripped the barrel in both hands. "Since you've brought it up, Tom, we should decide now whether we stick this out or mount and get out while we still can."

"I vote we stick," Tom replied.

"Milo?" Nate asked.

"Can I talk to Tom in private?"

"Of course."

The Pennsylvanians moved to the east and began arguing in harsh whispers.

"They will decide to stay," Red Moon said.

"I know," Nate responded.

"We are fools if we do."

"I know."

"And I am the biggest fool of all because I will not leave until they have all the hides our packhorses can carry. I need my share of the money for my grandson."

Nate grinned. "You're no bigger a fool than they are."

"How about you?"

"Do you think the thing will leave us alone?"

"No."

"Tom could be right. It might be wounded."

"Yes, but that will not stop it," Red Moon said. "The thing that lurks in the dark hates men. It will not rest until every one of us is dead or gone."

"Why hasn't it come after us? Why attack the Blackfeet first when there were more of them?"

The Crow looked at Samson. The dog was sniffing a corpse. "I do not know."

"But you think it has something to do with Samson?" Nate asked, and included the clearing in a sweep of his hand. "The creature can't be afraid of him." He frowned. "The creature can't be afraid of anything."

"It is not fear. Something else."

"What?" Nate probed, but the Pennsylvanians chose that moment to return.

"We've settled the issue," Tom declared.

"Yes," Milo agreed hesitantly. "We want to continue trapping."

"I too will stay," Red Moon stated.

Nate was suddenly the focus of attention. If he had any smarts he would tell them so long and ride as if the Devil himself was hot on his heels. But he'd given these men his word that he would trap the valley with them and they were counting on him to do his share of the work. If he left now, it would take them twice as long to do it all.

"What do you say, Nate?" Milo inquired.

"Yeah, King," Tom added. "I never took you for a quitter, but a man never knows. How do you vote?"

An invisible ghastly specter seemed to tug at Nate's soul and he felt a stab of cold deep within himself, but he ignored the disquieting sensation. In the certain knowledge of the sequence of events that would ensue, and with a full awareness of the implications for his future, Nate sighed and gave them his answer. "We keep trapping."

Chapter Sixteen

Somber and silent, the four men rode from the scene of slaughter to the junction of the forks in the stream. Each one of them rode with a rifle in hand, senses primed, eyes constantly in motion.

Milo and Tom were most affected. Where before they had frequently joked or sang or related outlandish tales they had heard, they were now grim, their lips compressed, the very postures of their bodies testifying to the nervous tension permeating every pore.

Before leaving the clearing, Red Moon had tracked the creature into the stream where the flowing water had erased its prints on the bottom. So they had no idea in which direction it had gone. Nor, from the few tracks found, could they determine if it had been wounded in the battle with the Blackfeet.

Nate, riding in the lead, noticed Samson seemed unusually alert too. He wondered if the dog sensed their state of mind or whether its own instinct for self-preservation had been aroused by the slaughter.

At the junction they turned and rode up the left fork. Because there were more trees along this fork and the undergrowth was exceptionally heavy near the water, much heavier than it had been up the right fork, they were unable to stick as close to the stream as they would have liked. They were forced to follow the path of least resistance, riding where the trees and brush were thin enough to permit their horses to pass without difficulty. Often they were dozens of yards from the gurgling fork, unable to note the location of beaver lodges and to plan where they would set their traps.

Nate's uneasiness had been eclipsed by constant razor-edged apprehension. He was jumpy and knew it, but he made no attempt to calm his jangled nerves. He well knew that when a man was on edge he was more aware of his surroundings and his reactions were quicker. And he might need that extra bit of wariness and speed should the beast come after them.

They had gone a quarter of a mile when Red Moon, who rarely spoke when they were on the trail, made an observation. "Few birds," he said. "Few squirrels and chipmunks."

Suddenly Nate realized a hush enveloped the forest through which they were passing. On the other fork there had been the continual twitter of birds and the chatter of squirrels and such. Now there was only an oppressive silence rarely broken by the normal forest sounds.

Where were all the small animals?

His mouth had gone dry and he worked his tongue back and forth, getting his saliva to flow again. He licked his lips and berated himself for being an idiot. By all rights he should be on his way to his cabin.

He came to a small clearing and bright sunlight stabbed into his eyes like a red-hot knife. The contrast between the gloomy forest and the clearing was startling. Squinting, he gazed at the trees, noting for the first time that the shadows were deeper and darker than they should be. He twisted in the saddle and peered upward at the regal mountain bordering the left fork on the opposite side of the stream. Over ten thousand feet high and rimmed with snow, the mountain was almost barren except along its lower slopes. It cast an enormous shadow over the entire left fork.

He looked closer. Much of the mountain between the low slopes and the snow consisted of a series of sheer cliffs rising to dizzying heights. Brilliant sunshine reflected off the tops of those cliffs. The lower portions, however, were obscured in inky shadow. He spied a circular patch of black below one cliff that might well be a cave, but the distance was too great for him to be certain.

Once across the clearing he paid attention to the undergrowth and trees hemming him in. If the creature sprang from concealment he would have a second or less to bring his weapons to bear. He must be ready at all times.

Hours went by. They didn't bother to stop for a noon rest. The sun climbed high into the sky, and not until late in the afternoon, when a meadow unfolded before them, did Nate halt and look at his companions.

"How about if we stop here for the night? It's still early, but we're all tired and the horses need a break."

"Fine with me," Milo said, arching his back. "I'd like to walk around and stretch my legs."

"We're awful far from the stream," Tom complained. "It must be two hundreds yards off."

Nate gazed at the intervening woods. Two hundred yards was a lot to cover when there might be an inhuman demon out there just waiting for an opportunity to pounce on one of them. "Since it's my idea to make camp here, I'll water the horses and fill our water bags," he offered.

"I will help you," Red Moon said.

They attended to their tasks with a minimum of conversation. After their saddles and supplies were stripped off their horses, Milo worked on their supper. Tom arranged their gear so it would be close at hand.

Nate took half of their animals and headed for the stream, Samson padding beside him. Red Moon, with the rest of the stock, came along.

The Crow kept looking through the trees toward the cliffs. "We do not need to worry until after the sun sets," he said. "Then the thing will begin to hunt."

"Maybe it ate its fill last night," Nate said. "Maybe it won't come out tonight."

"Maybe."

The dense brush necessitated hard work on their part before they pushed their way through to the water. Nate led his animals in first so Red Moon could stand guard.

Samson moved along the bank, sniffing the ground and testing the air.

"He knows," Red Moon said.

Nate was inclined to hurry the horses, but the animals had worked long and hard and deserved to drink their full. He stood in the stream, the water up to his ankles, and scanned the other side, bothered by a vague sensation of being watched. If the thing was there, he'd never know. The trees, high grass, and weeds presented an unbroken green wall extending for as far as the eye could see. There were also numerous thickets where a large animal could easily conceal itself. Spotting it would be a fluke.

Finally the last of Nate's animals raised its dripping muzzle and he took them onto the bank. Red Moon led the rest of the horses into the stream.

Nate watched the old Crow, thinking of the sacrifice the warrior was making to help his grandson. "My wife and I have some money put aside," he mentioned casually.

Red Moon glanced at him.

"If the worst should happen and we're driven out of the valley before we get enough hides, I'd be happy to give you the money you'll need to reach St. Louis."

The Crow lifted his rifle and became unusually interested in his ramrod. At length he replied in a husky voice. "Thank you, Grizzly Killer, I will keep it in mind."

Soon the horses were done and Nate took the lead back to the meadow. Milo was pouring coffee into a cup. Tom had gathered enough dead branches to last them a week and was still collecting more.

"See anything?" Milo asked.

"Peaceful as could be," Nate responded.

During the meal no one said a word. Each ate with his rifle in ready reach. The sun dipped below the western horizon and plunged the meadow into murky darkness.

Tom Sublette fed more limbs to the fire.

"Who wants first watch?" Nate inquired as the flames hissed and spit sparks into the cool air.

"Me," Milo promptly answered. "I doubt I can sleep much anyway."

"Me either," Tom said.

Nate took a sip from his fourth cup of coffee. He doubted whether he would sleep very much either. Somehow, he must. They all must. Fatigue made men careless, and a single mistake now could well cost any one of them his life.

It was then, as each man was lost in his own troubled thoughts, that a cry arose from the heights of the towering mountain beyond the stream, an eerie cry unlike that of any panther or other wild animal in existence, a drawn-out, wavering cry that rose in volume and diminished abruptly again and again without end.

"What the hell!" Tom blurted out at the first note, and grabbed for his rifle.

Nate stood and turned, his body tingling. It sounded more like a moan than a cry of rage, as if the creature making it was in acute misery.

"It's the thing," Milo said breathlessly.

"It is hurt," Red Moon stated.

On and on the cry lingered until, minutes later, it was replaced by the subtle rustling of the breeze in the trees.

Milo took two steps away from the fire. "That thing must be up there right this minute watching us. It knows we're here."

"That was just the wind," Tom said.

"You know better," Milo replied.

Rising, Tom nodded at the black bulk of the mountain that loomed above them like a menacing giant. "Get a grip on yourself. At times we've both heard the wind whistling through the high peaks. It can make all kinds of sounds."

"Not like that," Milo said.

"It's the wind," Tom insisted.

No one else believed him. Nate could see that. He also guessed that Tom didn't believe it himself. So why was Sublette being so stubborn? Couldn't he face the truth? Or was Tom simply afraid and unwilling to acknowledge his fear?

Red Moon drew a blanket over his shoulders. "It would be wise to have two men stay on guard at a time," he mentioned.

Nate agreed. If one should doze off the other could rouse him. "All right. Milo and Tom, take the first watch, then wake Red Moon and me." He finished the coffee, made himself comfortable in his blankets, and closed his eyes. Despite his weariness, he doubted he would sleep a wink. He couldn't, not with that thing up on the heights above them. Not in a million years.

A firm hand on his shoulder brought Nate around. He blinked and sat up, gazing in bewilderment at the low fire. "What is it?" he asked drowsily.

"The night is half done," Milo told him. "It's your turn to stand guard."

Half done? Nate tilted his head to see the stars in the heavens and recognized from the position of the Big Dipper that Benteen was right. He'd slept after all, for hours, but he felt no more refreshed than he had when he'd lain down. In fact, he felt worse. His muscles ached and his bladder was about to burst.

Red Moon was pouring coffee for both of them.

"The night has been quiet," Milo reported. "Once we thought we heard something moving through the brush to the north of us, but the crackling stopped."

Yawning, Nate rose. He swung his arms in circles and stamped his legs to get his blood flowing.

"Where's your dog, King?" Tom asked.

Pivoting, Nate searched the grass revealed in the flickering firelight but saw no sign of Samson. "I don't know," he said uncertainly. "I thought he was right at my side when I fell asleep."

"We noticed he was gone about an hour ago," Milo disclosed. "Didn't think too much of it at the time because he's always wandering off when the mood strikes him."

"But not at night," Nate said, anger flaring at their neglect in not letting him know sooner. "Why didn't you wake me?"

Milo shrugged. "We didn't think it was important. Sorry."

Nate inserted two fingers into his mouth and whistled shrilly, hoping the dog would return. He'd never had cause to whistle to it before so he didn't know what it would do. If he was lucky, the dog's previous owner had taught it to respond to whistling. He waited expectantly, hearing only the wind.

"Samson might be a mile off by now," Milo said. "Perhaps he didn't hear you."

Undaunted, Nate whistled again, even louder than the first time. Again he waited.

"Try once more," Milo urged after a while.

The whistle pierced the night, louder than the hoot of an owl or the screech of a bird of prey, carried by the wind across the valley to the steep slopes of the massive mountain. A minute went by. Then two.

Nate stooped to retrieve his Hawken. "Keep the fires going. I'll be back as soon as I find Samson."

"You're not going out there?" Milo asked in amazement.

Nodding, Nate took a stride, but the old Crow barred his path.

"It would be foolish, Grizzly Killer, to go into the forest before daylight. The thing that lurks in the dark might be waiting for one of us to make such a mistake. Samson can take care of himself."

Nate paused. Red Moon made sense, but he was loathe to stand idle when the dog might need him. He'd grown attached to the mutt over the past few weeks and he intended to take it back to the cabin and surprise Winona and Zach.

"Yeah," Tom chimed in. "I don't care much for the dog, but we can't stand to lose you. So stay here and wait for the mangy sack of fur."

Opening his mouth to issue a sharp retort, Nate froze when from the cliffs high above them there came a whistle in every respect exactly like his own.

Chapter Seventeen

"My God!" Milo exclaimed.

"It must be an echo," Tom said.

Spinning, Milo glared at his friend. "Damn your hide! You know what's up there as well as we do! It's not the wind, and it's not an echo."

"Has to be an echo," Tom stubbornly argued. "Since when do animals whistle like we do?"

Another whistle wafted down from the high elevations, distinct in the crisp mountain air, a perfect copy of Nate's own whistling only louder.

Milo faced the Crow warrior. "What the hell is up there?" he demanded in a strained voice. "What are we up against?"

"I wish I could tell you. No one has ever seen the beast and lived."

"You must know more. There must be something you're not telling us," Milo said, and jabbed a finger at the mountain. "How can a mere animal rout twenty

Blackfeet? How can an animal whistle like that?" He paused, his fists clenched, shaking from the intensity of his emotion. "What the hell *is* it?"

Red Moon bowed his head.

"I've had enough," Milo snapped, glancing at Sublette. "I don't care what you say. We're fools if we stay. Let's mount up and ride out before it's too late."

Tom stepped over and put a hand on Benteen's shoulder. "What's gotten into you? We have an agreement."

"To hell with the agreement!" Milo roared. "Didn't you see the bodies of those poor Blackfeet? Didn't you see their crushed skulls and busted limbs? Whatever killed them is a monster! A living, breathing monster that will do the same thing to us unless we leave this valley." He stared at the peaks, his eyes wide. "That's it! That's the answer! The thing calls this valley home and it doesn't like intruders. If we leave we'll be safe. It won't follow us. I know it."

"I'm not leaving," Tom said softly.

Milo whirled, his face creased in stark disbelief. "Weren't you listening to me? We must go."

"Listen to yourself," Tom said. "You were all set to fight it out with a Blackfoot war party when we were badly outnumbered, but now you're willing to turn tail, to turn your back on a fortune in prime pelts because of a lowly animal?"

"We don't know if it is an animal."

"What else, then? A ghost? Ghosts don't crush skulls and rip arms from bodies. This thing is flesh and blood like you and me, and like us it can be killed. All it takes is a well-placed ball in its head."

Nate saw Milo frown, saw sorrowful resignation in the man's eyes, and he felt sorry for him. Milo knew they were making the biggest mistake of their lives by staying, but he couldn't convince his best friend. And since they were good friends, Milo couldn't very well ride off and leave Sublette to face the creature alone. Milo was trapped by his friendship, just as Nate was committed because he had given his word and Red Moon because of his ailing grandson. All three wanted to leave. None of them could.

"If you say so," Milo said to Tom in a forlorn fashion. Stepping to his bedroll, he rolled out his blankets and turned in without another word, cradling his rifle in his arms.

Tom made a clucking noise in reproach, then also spread out his blankets. After lying on his back he placed his right forearm over his eyes, and within a minute he sound asleep.

Coffee was in order, Nate decided, savoring the stimulating taste, his gaze roving over the meadow. The horses were all at rest. Nothing moved in the trees. Although he listened intently, he did not hear the whistle repeated.

For the rest of the night Nate drank coffee to keep himself awake and paced around the camp, seldom standing still for more than a few seconds. Worry over Samson bothered him and he longed to see the big dog loping toward him from the forest.

Eventually dawn created a crimson blaze in the sky to the east. Normally, the birds would rouse to life and chirp gaily to greet the new day. But here, in the oppressive shadow of the sinister mountain, few did so. A robin here. A sparrow there. For the most part the forest was as silent as a tomb.

Nate woke up Benteen and Sublette. Neither was in a pleasant frame of mind. Milo grumbled a sour "Good morning." Tom scowled at the world in general. All four of them huddled around the fire to drink coffee and munch on jerked venison.

At last Milo said, "Do we continue up the stream or should we begin trapping right where we are?"

"We go upstream," Tom responded. "Why start here

when we're only about halfway up the fork? Think of all the beaver we'll lose."

"I'm thinking of staying alive," Milo said.

"Now don't start again."

Nate could see an argument blossoming. He held up a hand to draw their attention. "Why don't we compromise? We can use this spot as our base camp for a while and trap the stream in both directions. If all goes well, if we trap for a couple of days and the thing that killed the Blackfeet doesn't give us any trouble, we can press on to the end of the fork."

"I like the idea," Milo said.

"Well, I don't," Tom declared. "But I know better than to waste my breath trying to change your minds. If you promise me that we'll go up the fork once we've caught all the beaver there are in this stretch of the stream, I'll agree."

"I said we would," Nate reminded him.

"All right. Milo and I will lay our traps northwest of the camp. The Crow and you can lay yours to the southeast," Tom proposed.

Nate's temper flared. "The Crow, as you constantly refer to him, has a name."

"And we all know what it is, don't we?" Tom retorted. Upending his coffee cup over the fire as he rose, he glanced at Benteen. "Come on, Milo. I find the company here as stale as week-old bread." He walked off to the pile of trapping gear.

"Sorry, Nate," Milo said, and trailed his companion.

Nate waited until they departed, each burdened with six traps, before he put his cup down and opened the pack containing his Newhouses. He issued a half dozen to Red Moon, took six for himself, then remembered to completely extinguish the fire before making for the stream.

They emerged from the undergrowth close to a large beaver damn. Nate found a likely spot and placed his first Newhouse of the day. Sticking close to the water's edge, they hiked southeast and took turns positioning the rest of their traps. By the time they were done the sun was almost to the midday position. Not once had they seen or heard anything out of the ordinary.

Nate lent Red Moon a hand in climbing out of the frigid water after the Crow set the final one. "Let's go hunting after we reach camp," he suggested. "I'm tired of jerky, and since the beast knows we're here there's no reason not to fire our guns."

"Fresh elk meat would be nice."

About to agree, Nate gazed at the brush on the far side and spied movement in a thicket. Every muscle in his body tensed. He swung the Hawken to his shoulder, cocked the hammer, and took a bead on a dark form flitting through the vegetation toward the water.

"Don't shot," Red Moon said.

From between two pines near the water appeared Samson. He spotted them instantly and without hesitation plunged into the gently flowing water. His legs kicking in powerful strokes, he swam toward where they stood.

Relief made Nate smile. Dropping to one knee, he gestured for the dog to keep coming. "That's it, boy," he encouraged. "You're doing fine."

"Something follows the dog," Red Moon said.

Nate glanced at the forest rimming the opposite bank, his blood turning cold at the sight of the same thicket through which Samson had passed now swaying from side to side as something else moved through it. Standing, he clutched the Hawken and waited for whatever it was to show itself. But the thicket stopped moving and all was still.

"It watches us," Red Moon declared.

"Do you see it?"

"No. But I know."

Nate longed for a glimpse of the creature, just

enough to see what it was. He thought he saw a pine tree shake, but the motion ceased so abruptly he wasn't sure.

Splashing loudly, Samson reached the shore and clambered onto the bank. He paused to shake himself, spraying water in all directions.

Some drops spattered on Nate's face. He tore his eyes from the far bank so he could give the dog an affectionate rub under the chin. "Where have you been?" he demanded as if talking to an errant child. "I've been worried about you."

"We should leave, Grizzly Killer," Red Moon said.

Nate nodded. Benteen and Sublette should be told that the creature had descended from the heights and was in the area. He backed from the stream until he bumped against a tree, then spun and hurried for camp. Samson stayed close to him. Where *had* the dog gone? he wondered. Up the mountain? Why? Had it somehow trailed the creature by scent to its lair, and then the beast had followed Samson back down? No, that couldn't be. The creature would have killed Samson.

At length he saw the meadow through the trees and hastened his pace. He was still 20 yards off when he perceived that all was not well. First he noticed the horses. They were bunched together, their heads up, their ears pricked, their attention on the woods to the northwest. Then, through a gap in the trees, the camp itself came into view.

Nate halted in alarm. The contents of their packs lay all over the ground! He placed his right hand on a flintlock and broke into a run, bursting from the brush onto a scene of total, wanton destruction.

Every pack, every parflache, every pouch had been upended. The food had been trampled into the dust. Their clothes and blankets had been shredded and scattered about. The water bags had been torn apart.

and flung aside. Even worse, many of their pelts had been ripped in half. And an axe handle had been broken in two as a man might snap a twig.

"The beast did this," Red Moon said.

"How?" Nate responded in exasperation. "It was behind us. How did it do this?" He moved among the debris, seeking anything that could be salvaged. But the creature had done a thorough job of destroying every last article they possessed. Even the coffeepot had been smashed.

To the northwest there arose a crashing in the forest as something barreled through the brush toward their camp

The thing! Nate's mind shrieked, and he whirled with the Hawken leveled. A running figure materialized, a figure in buckskins, and seconds later Milo Benteen dashed into the open. He took several paces, spotted them, and halted. His breath came in great gasps. There were thin cuts on his cheeks where the brush had lashed his face, and his hat was gone.

"Milo?" Nate said, running over to him. "What is it? What happened?" He looked into the forest. "Where's Tom?"

Benteen inhaled raggedly and tried to speak but failed. His features were pale, almost the color of milk. He motioned to his rear and croaked, "Gone. Tom is gone."

"What do you mean?" Nate asked, grasping the terrified man by the arm. "Tell us what happened!"

"The thing," Milo said, tears forming in his eyes. "The thing," he repeated softly, and sank to his knees, his head bowed.

Nate hefted his rifle and came to an immediate decision. "I'm going after Tom," he told Red Moon. "You stay here and try to bring Milo around."

"Be careful."

"You too. Keep an eye on the trees," Nate advised.

He leaned down and shook Milo. "Where did you see Tom last?"

Benteen stared blankly at the grass and didn't answer.

"How far up the stream did you go?" Nate persisted.

"He is in shock," Red Moon said.

"Damn," Nate muttered, and took off in the direction of the stream. He checked to verify Samson was tagging along, then ran all out, bounding over logs and skirting trees and thickets, the Hawken always gripped in both hands. He knew the thing was close by. He could feel it in his bones. A lapse of alertness now would spell his certain death.

He reached the fork and stopped. In the soft earth next to the stream were two sets of tracks, both moccasin prints. Tom and Milo had been moving upstream seeking places to put their traps.

In order to make better time, Nate jumped into the water and then ventured upstream. The undergrowth hugging the bank dipped low in many spots, nearly touching the surface, and he shied well clear of those points, wary of being jumped by the beast. Trailing the Pennsylvanians was simplicity itself. They'd made no effort to hide their tracks and there were many in evidence at the water's edge. He came to where they had placed their first trap, and halted.

Something had wrenched the stake from the earth, hauled the trap out, and bent the heavy steel as if it had been mere paper. The crumpled contraption now lay on the bank, completely useless. A partial print in the mud told the story.

Nate realized the creature had been shadowing the Pennsylvanians, observing them lay the trap line. After they had set this one and gone on, it had probably waited until they were out of sight and then slipped from concealment to do its dirty work. He studied the trap and discovered the jaws had been sprung prior to being twisted into so much useless metal. The beast must have used a stick to push the disk down and release the trigger.

He straightened in astonishment. There were many tales of wolves and wolverines that had raided trap lines and taken dead beaver off to eat, but in those instances the beaver were always torn from the traps and parts of their bodies were still held fast by the closed jaws. Never had he heard of an animal deliberately springing a trap. The creature must have done so to prevent the jaws from closing on it when it twisted the metal.

Nate stared at the forest, staggered by the discovery. This thing—this fiend—must be extraordinarily intelligent, far more intelligent than any animal he'd ever encountered. He dared not underestimate its intellect.

Samson began testing the air with his nose.

What did the dog smell? Nate surveyed the forest on both sides but saw no cause for concern. He headed up the stream again, his feet soaked to the ankles. In due course he found a second trap lying on the bank of a beaver pond. This trap had been accorded the same treatment as the first.

The tracks of Milo and Tom were still fresh. Apparently they'd had no idea they were being pursued. Now and then they'd position a Newhouse and go on. Exercising stealth and cunning the creature had closed in, gradually overtaking them.

Nate tramped for over three miles and spotted seven ruined traps. Then he rounded a bend and saw a tributary on his side of the stream, a narrow creek wending off among the trees. At the junction he stopped and scoured the ground.

The tracks told the story. Milo and Tom had halted and talked, and one of them had gone off up the tributary, perhaps to check for beaver. From the length of the stride and size of the footprints of the man who had gone to investigate the creek, Nate knew Tom had volunteered to handle the chore. Milo had continued up the stream, finished setting the traps, and returned. He'd promptly proceeded along the creek at a rapid clip, no doubt worried because Tom hadn't met him at the junction.

Nate gave Samson a pat on the head and jogged along the creek bank. The brush was thinner and he made good time. In a quarter of a mile he came to a beaver pond and saw a lodge out in the water. The tracks of Sublette and Benteen circled the pond so he did the same until he stood beside a damn where he halted to study the terrain.

Tom Sublette was straight ahead.

Nate stiffened on seeing the stocky form of the Pennsylvanian seated in front of a log near the water. Sublette's arms were draped casually at his sides, his rifle resting across his thighs. The shadow of a towering pine partially obscured Sublette's head and shoulders, and Nate couldn't tell in which direction the man was looking. "Tom!" he cried.

Sublette didn't move or acknowledge the hail.

Fearing the worst, Nate ran forward, covering almost the entire 30 feet before the awful truth drew him up short in unspeakable horror. He gaped, finally seeing the ragged flesh rimming the neck and the flies buzzing greedily about.

It was Tom Sublette, all right.

But just his body.

His head was gone.

Chapter Eighteen

Stunned, Nate cautiously advanced. Goose flesh broke out all over his body and his scalp tingled. Samson glided past him and sniffed Sublette's feet, then growled.

Evidently Tom had hiked this far and sat down to rest, his spine braced against the log, his back to the deep woods. How long he had sat there was impossible to gauge, but clearly long enough for the creature to slink out of hiding, creep up on the unsuspecting man, and tear Tom's head off. Strips of skin hung like tiny flaps over the collar of his buckskin shirt. Because of the copious blood that had spurted out when the head was ripped off, the shirt had been dyed a shade of pink.

Nate suppressed an impulse to be sick. He glanced at the log and slowly inched up to it. Beyond lay the missing head.

Tom's visage was oddly tranquil, as if death had

seized him before he was aware of the creature's horrid grip. Perhaps, Nate reasoned, the end had come swiftly.

He noticed a hole in the top of the head and leaned down for a closer examination. Again his stomach heaved and he drew back, appalled to his core. The top of Tom's head had been peeled back in the same manner as an orange and the contents of his cranial cavity scooped out. Nate looked for the brain but saw no sign of it. A grisly idea occurred to him and he shuddered.

At that moment, faint but audible, from the vicinity of the meadow came the retort of a rifle.

The camp was under attack! Nate pivoted, darted around the log, and raced off. Instead of following the stream, which entailed taking a circuitous route, he made a beeline for the meadow. He plowed through heavy brush and thickets, using the Hawken to batter a path where the vegetation was especially dense, oblivious to the many tiny branches that bit into his face and neck. All he could think of was Red Moon and Milo. They were in dire danger and he must reach them before the beast did to them what it had done to Tom and the Blackfeet.

He thought of those unfortunate Blackfeet again, of how a single creature had dispatched nearly the entire war party, and he was troubled by an aspect to the attack he felt he was overlooking. He couldn't isolate the reason, but something bothered him.

The distance seemed unending. He fought his way through tangled undergrowth time and again. Once his leg was hooked by a low limb and he fell, jarring his elbows in the process. He surged upright and raced on, ignoring the pain.

No other gunshots sounded. He began to think he was mistaken, that Red Moon had been out hunting game for their supper and had downed a deer or an elk. If the creature had attacked, surely the Crow and Milo would have gotten off more than one shot.

Over a mile from the creek he slowed, tuckered out, to conserve his breath and his energy. He thought of Samson, and glanced over his shoulder to see if the dog was still with him.

Samson had vanished.

Nate paused, but only for a second. His friends needed him. The dog could take care of itself and would show up when it was ready. Squaring his broad shoulders, he continued to run, pacing himself so he wouldn't be completely exhausted when he reached the meadow. If the creature was there he would need all of his strength and wits to dispatch it.

Sweat poured down his back and legs. He felt drops trickle down his cheek. His legs muscles protested the marathon but he forged ahead. Soon he would be there. Soon he would know.

It turned out he had miscalculated. The trees were to his rear and green grass was underfoot before he realized he'd emerged from the forest at the north end of the meadow instead of the south, where their camp was situated. He stopped, taking loud breaths, and saw with a sinking sensation in his gut that the horses were gone, every last one of them. They had yanked out their picket pins and galloped off.

Smoke curled skyward from the fire. He sprinted closer, seeking his companions. Their ruined supplies were still lying all over the place. Neither Red Moon nor Milo was anywhere in sight.

Nate stopped and wiped first one palm, then the other, on his leggings. "Red Moon?" he called, hoping against hope for a reply. "Milo? Where are you?"

Utter quiet prevailed in the meadow and the encircling forest.

"Red Moon?" Nate repeated, slowly stepping nearer to the fire, the stock of the Hawken flush with his shoulder. His thumb rested on the hammer, his finger lightly touched the trigger. "Red—" he began, and then beheld the body lying at the tree line to the south of the camp.

He surveyed the woods around him and drew abreast of the fire. To his left he saw Milo's long gun, the stock shattered, the heavy barrel bent.

In the forest to the west something snarled.

Nate stopped in mid-stride and swung around, expecting to see the beast charge from cover. Nothing happened, though, and he resumed walking to the body.

It was Milo, prone with his arms out flung. His face, twisted sideways, revealed a countenance locked in unparalleled fear. There were four fangs marks on his neck, blood still trickling from the punctures. From the unusual angle at which his head lay, it was easy to see his neck had been broken.

"Oh, Milo," Nate said softly. He studied the tracks, and read how Milo had been fleeing toward the trees when the creature overtook him from the rear. Poor Milo had not had a chance. In Milo's panic, he must have discarded his gun back near the fire.

Nate turned from side to side, seeking Red Moon. The Crow must be nearby, perhaps dead, perhaps wounded. Red Moon would not die easily, and that shot he'd heard must have been the warrior selling his life dearly. He moved along the tree line, searching for footprints. Ten yards from Milo's body he found moccasin prints leading into the forest. From the length of the stride, he concluded Red Moon had been running.

He peered into the gloomy woods, the gravity of his predicament hitting home. For all he knew, he was now alone. The horses were gone, leaving him stranded afoot hundreds of miles from his cabin. Even if he escaped from the valley he must cover a tremendous distance in a land teeming with grizzlies and wolves and panthers. Not to mention the Blackfeet. Few trappers left on foot lived to tell the tale. He would be lucky if he ever laid eyes on Winona and Zach again.

A moan issued from the forest, seeming to come from near a large pine 25 yards away.

Red Moon? Or the creature? Nate entered the woods, keeping low, stepping with extreme care to avoid twigs and branches that might break underfoot and give his position away. If the thing jumped him he would put up the fight of his life. He had the Hawken, the two flintlocks, and his butcher knife. There was plenty of ammunition in his ammo pouch and his powder horn was filled to the brim. He'd give a good account of himself before he died.

Every shadow seemed menacing. Any movement, no matter how slight, set his nerves on edge. If a leaf fluttered, he froze.

The oppressive silence gnawed at him, increasing his jumpiness. He recalled the Indian legends about the thing that lurked in the dark. Here it was broad daylight, and the beast was abroad and on the rampage. So much for the reliability of legends. Or had the Indians meant the dark of the forest and not the dark of night?

He shook his head, dispelling the foolish conjecture. If he allowed himself to be distracted the creature would find him easy pickings. Moving ever closer to the pine, he listened for another moan. When he was 15 feet off he heard one, low and brief. He thought it came from somewhere on his right and he headed in that direction. There were a number of trees growing quite near to one another with thick growth filling gaps among the trunks. On silent feet he slid in among them and stopped.

His head snapped up when he heard a peculiar

noise, a slight tap-tap-tap as if someone was rapping on a tree. He cocked his head, striving to pinpoint where the noise originated, and happened to spy a leaf lying on the ground. As his gaze fell on it a crimson drop fell from on high and hit the leaf, then another and another. This was the tapping he had heard.

Nate inched forward and looked into the tree above the leaf. An inarticulate cry passed from his lips and he rose, dazed, his mind whirling.

Red Moon hung six feet above the ground. He had been bodily lifted and impaled on a broken branch, and the bloody point of the branch protruded seven or eight inches from his chest. His arms and legs dangled limply. Blood flowed from the wound, down over his shirt and leggings, and dripped from the heel of his moccasins. His head sagged, his eyes were closed.

"No," Nate said. "Dear Lord, no."

The Crow's eyes flicked wide but it was a moment before he focused. He saw Nate and struggled to move his mouth until a word rasped out. "Run."

"I can't leave you," Nate said, touching Red Moon on the leg. "I'll try and get you down from there."

"No," the warrior said. "The beast has killed me. Save yourself. Get away before it comes."

"I won't desert you," Nate insisted.

Out of the depths of a thicket to the north came a piercing shriek of bestial rage and the thicket shook as if in a violent wind.

Nate's reaction was instinctive. He pivoted, took hasty aim, and fired into the center of the branches shaking the hardest. The shriek broke off and the underbrush crackled as something retreated through the forest.

"Run," Red Moon said.

"Save your breath," Nate responded, already beginning to reload. First he placed the butt of the rifle on the ground. Then his hands flew as he measured out the proper amount of black powder from his powder horn into his palm and fed the powder down the barrel. Next he took a ball from his ammo pouch and wrapped the ball in a wad. The ramrod came out easily, and after inserting the ball and wad into the end of the muzzle he used the ramrod to force both down on top of the powder. It took no time at all to replace the ramrod in its housing under the barrel. Turning, he looked up at his friend.

Red Moon had died. His eyes were open but blank, his mouth slack, a tinge of sadness lining his face.

"I won't let you down," Nate said softly. Facing due south, he ran. Ran as he had never run before. For the next hour and a half he maintained a grueling, steady pace that an Apache would have been proud of, a dogtrot that ate up the miles. He steeled his mind to the pain in his legs. All that mattered was putting distance between himself and the creature. If he traveled far enough, if he could get close to the valley entrance before weariness prevented him from going any further, he just might get out of the valley in one piece.

He thought often of his shot into the thicket, and consoled himself with the idea he'd wounded the beast. If so, like any animal it would go to its lair or seek an isolated place to hole up and lick the wound. Or so he hoped.

The afternoon sun climbed steadily higher, causing the temperature to rise. He sweated profusely and his soaked buckskins clung to his frame. When he came to where the forks merged he turned and followed the main stream. Here the going was easier and he stayed near the water so he could quench his thirst whenever the need became too overpowering.

Nate often scanned his back trail. As the hours elapsed and he continued to see no indication of pursuit he let himself relax a trifle. His legs were afire with pain. From his hips to the soles of his feet he was in constant discomfort. Years of living in the wilderness had bestowed remarkable endurance on him, but even superbly conditioned muscles possessed limits. When he could stand it no longer, he halted.

The stream beckoned invitingly. He shuffled over and sank to his knees, then splashed handfuls of the refreshing liquid on his face and neck. The water trickled under his shirt and down his chest, cooling his overheated body.

Nate touched his lips to the stream and drank sparingly. Too much water might sicken him. When a man was on the verge of exhaustion and had sweated practically every spare drop of moisture from his body, it was best to take small sips and slowly slake the craving for water. Later he could drink to his heart's content—provided he lived long enough.

He stood and stared northward. Where in the world was Samson? The dog had always been independent-minded, but it sure had picked a hell of a time to begin traipsing off wherever its whim led it. Samson's superior senses would come in handy right about now and he sorely missed the dog.

The sun drew his attention. There was no way he could reach the valley entrance before nightfall. If all went well he'd arrive there sometime tomorrow, about mid-morning. Which meant he must spend another anxious night in the domain of the wicked devil that would no doubt be stalking him once the sun dipped from sight.

He resumed running, but slowly to conserve his strength. In the few hours before twilight he could cover another four or five miles. Then he must find a place to make a stand.

Yet his options were limited. He could climb a tree and spend the night high in its branches, but he'd be unable to get a good night's rest and he badly needed rest if he wanted to flee the valley swiftly in the morning. He could dig a hole and crawl in, but for all he knew the creature tracked by scent and would find him without difficulty.

No, he needed another idea.

By the time he'd gone almost five miles and the sun had started its inexorable slide to the far side of the planet, he'd figured out what he would do. It was a simple plan, yet it might save his life.

He halted, drank some water, and stepped to the trees. There were plenty of broken limbs scattered around and he searched until he found three straight branches over five feet long, two of which had forked ends. Moving close to the stream again, he jammed the tapered end of one of the forked branches into the soil until it stood by itself, and then repeated the tactic with a second limb, placing it four feet from the first. Aligning the last limb in the forks of the uprights took but a moment.

Back to the forest he went to gather an arm-load of long, slender branches. These he leaned on the make-shift cross-beam to his lean-to in a neat row. Then he found smaller, even thinner branches, and weaved these among the longer branches to form a crude but serviceable wall facing to the north.

He collected more limbs and leaned these against the open end of the lean-to, leaving only a narrow space on either side to gain entry. This was deliberate. Should the beast hunt him down, it would have to tear the limbs aside to get at him. The noise was bound to awaken him and perhaps give him time to bring his guns to bear.

As an extra precaution he again ventured into the woods and gathered all the dry leaves and small dead twigs he could find. These he scattered in a wide circle around the lean-to until he had formed a carpet of crunchy material that would snap and crackle when stepped on.

Nate stood back and regarded his handiwork with satisfaction. The creature could not possibly reach him without making considerable noise, and a second or two of advance warning was all he needed to cock his rifle or pistols. It was the best he could do given the circumstances.

His stomach growled, but the sun was almost gone. He couldn't risk trying to find game. Instead, he eased to his hands and knees and crawled into the lean-to. Lying flat on his back so he could roll either way when the time came, he drew up his legs, rested the Hawken across his chest, and closed his eyes. His exertions had taken a terrible toll and fatigue washed over him from head to toe. He needed to sleep but doubted he could. Worry over the creature would keep him awake through the night. He thought of his dead friends and frowned. They never should have traveled to this vile valley, never should have let the lure of money eclipse their better judgment. He hoped Winona would forgive him if he never returned and hoped little Zach would retain some memory of his . . .

Nate opened his eyes with a start and held perfectly still, listening. He'd fallen asleep! For how long? He bent his head to see out the nearest opening. The night was pitch black except for the many stars dotting the sky, and a stiff wind from the northeast was bending the upper limbs of the trees. He had the feeling he'd dozed for hours but he couldn't be certain. His muscles ached, particularly those in his legs, and he still felt extremely tired. He was surprised he'd woken up at all.

Outside, dried leaves crunched.

Instantly Nate sat up, scarcely breathing, his fingers fumbling for the Hawken and closing on the barrel. Something was out there! He heard the stealthy pad of a step, heard more leaves crackle, and quickly cocked his rifle. The metallic click sounded loud enough to rouse a corpse. For a minute afterward the night was silent, then whatever was out there came closer to the lean-to.

Was it Samson? Nate hoped. Suddenly he could hear heavy breathing and knew it wasn't the dog. The creature had stalked him and was now out there, not more than a few feet away, perhaps baffled by the lean-to and trying to make sense of the structure. Nate peered at the opening opposite his feet.

The wind increased, whipping the trees, and the shaking leaves made enough noise to muffle the creature's steps.

A foul odor assailed Nate's nostrils, so rank it made him want to sneeze. He took his hand from the Hawken to pinch his nose tight, suppressing the impulse. In front of his eyes a great bulk loomed beyond the opening and a huge, hairy hand or paw reached inside. Dropping his hand to the rifle, he slanted the barrel at the beast and fired from the hip.

Flame and lead rent the darkness and a fierce howl filled the night. The looming bulk vanished, followed by the sound of something splashing across the stream.

Nate drew his right flintlock and moved to the opening. Near the far bank reared an enormous figure, well over seven feet in height, water spraying out from under its feet with every stride. It reached the far bank and disappeared in the undergrowth.

A second howl seemed to echo off the high cliffs above.

Elated, Nate commenced reloading the Hawken. The shot had driven the beast off! It could be killed just like any other animal. If he stayed awake he would be able to hold out until morning. He carefully poured black powder into his palm, having to guess at the proper amount by feel alone, and listened to a third howl from across the stream.

As if in response, from the forest close at hand came a shrill, bestial shriek.

A shiver rippled down Nate's spine and he glanced in that direction. There were two of the things! A high-pitched wail from off to the north indicated there were three, perhaps more. Shocked, he sat still while his mind raced. Now he understood how the Blackfeet had been wiped out. The creatures must have hit the war party from several directions all at once and slaughtered the confused braves before the Blackfeet could rally.

He continued reloading while pondering. If all three beasts attacked simultaneously, he'd be overrun and slain in moments. Oh, he might get one shot off, but the others would be on him before he could fire again. Creatures that size would be able to plow through the sides of the lean-to with no effort whatsoever.

Instead of feeling safe, he now felt boxed in. The lean-to was flimsy and his carpets of leaves wouldn't do much good if the creatures came in a concerted rush. His warning time would be next to nothing.

Nate finished reloading, then poked his head outside. The air was cool and invigorating, the night deceptively tranquil. Lurking somewhere out there were the beasts; they might be closing in already. He had a decision to make and he must make it swiftly.

Rising into a crouch, he tip-toed away from the lean-to, heading south along the stream. Maybe the things wouldn't notice, he told himself. Maybe they would think he was still inside. It might give him time to gain a substantial lead.

When he had gone 50 yards he straightened and ran full speed, heedless of the risk of stepping into a hole or tripping over an obstacle and seriously injuring himself. He had no intention of stopping for more than a brief rest until he reached the valley entrance. Once he was safely out the creatures might leave him alone.

The ammo pouch and powder horn slapped against his body as he ran, while the big knife smacked against his leg. He held the Hawken firmly in his left hand, swinging it at his side. Every so often he would press down on the flintlocks with his right hand, ensuring the pistols were snug under his wide leather belt.

He lost all track of time. After a mile or so his sore muscles loosened up and the stiffness went out of his joints. A minor pain intermittently flared in his chest but he disregarded it. Twice he stopped to gulp a mouthful of water and take a short breather.

A gray streak creased the eastern horizon when Nate spied, far ahead, the gap in the mountains that would grant him safety. He was winded again, so he halted and bent over, catching his breath.

Across the stream in the brush branches crackled as something moved about.

Straightening, Nate swung around and pressed the Hawken to his shoulder. A large, vague shape walked into the open and the creature seemed to be staring at him. He wondered if the things could see in the dark, like cats. If so, they had seen him sneak away from the lean-to.

A hint of sound to his rear made Nate whirl, his thumb pulling back on the hammer as he did. He saw a huge beast rushing at him, its arms outspread to envelop him in its crushing grip, its features veiled by the darkness except for its yellow fangs. Only a few yards separated them when Nate squeezed off a shot.

The ball took the creature low down, in the abdomen, the impact stopping it dead in its tracks. It doubled over, voiced a feral snarl, and leaped.

Nate tried to evade the thing's brawny arms but it clipped him on the right shoulder and knocked him to the earth. On hands and knees he glanced up at its great hairy bulk and saw it raise a fist overhead to pound him into the dirt. Another snarl sounded, only this one came from off to one side, and a black streak hurtled out of the night onto the creature.

Nate recognized that black streak and his resolve soared. Samson had come to his rescue! He saw the dog clamp its jaws on the beast's left wrist and the creature roared in primal fury, then swatted at Samson as a man might swat a fly. Nate heard the thud as the blow landed and imagined he heard the crack of Samson's ribs. Unless he came to the dog's aid, Samson would be slain.

He whipped both flintlocks out and up, cocking them as he drew. Pointing the left pistol at the creature's head, he fired. In the flash from the gun the beast's face was momentarily illuminated. Nate saw hairy, in-human features dominated by a pair of dark, sinister eyes, eyes seemingly aflame with unbridled hatred, and then the flash was gone and the beast bellowed in agony and flung Samson to the hard ground.

The creature spun, both hands or paws clasped to its face, and bounded into the forest, crashing through the undergrowth as it fled.

Nate twisted and spied the beast across the stream advancing toward him. It was a third of the way into the water and taking strides that no man could hope to match. He aimed hastily and fired his other flintlock.

Jerking around, the creature staggered, then re-covered and retreated, snarling and growling and rumbling in its barrel of a chest. Upon reaching the bank it bounded into the vegetation and fell silent.

Nate began reloading his guns, glancing in both di-rections in case the beasts came at him again. Samson rose, favoring a front leg, and limped over. His tongue flicked out and stroked Nate's cheek. "You pick a hell of a time to be affectionate," he muttered, his hands working feverishly.

Once all three weapons were ready, Nate jammed the pistols under his belt, grabbed the Hawken, and stood. Total quiet reigned in the woods on both sides of the stream, which meant nothing. The creatures might be skulking toward him at that very moment. Turning, he headed toward the gap at a slow gait so Samson could keep up without straining that injured leg too much. Splashes of red and yellow and orange colored the eastern sky. Soon the sun would rise.

They traveled half a mile when Nate glimpsed an indistinct form in the forest to his left. He halted and spun, dreading another onslaught but determined to fight until he dropped. Samson simply stood and stared, and Nate didn't understand why until a few seconds later when the thing in the trees came toward them.

Into the growing light stepped his stallion.

Epilogue

There were eight Crow women gathering berries on a low knoll less than a quarter of a mile from their village. They chatted as they worked, gossiping about the latest news of a raid the men had been on against the Utes.

Stiff Back Woman was the oldest in the group. She had gotten her name in childhood when an accident had rendered her incapable of bending over. A horse had kicked her squarely between the shoulder blades and she had never been the same. Still, she had led a good life. She'd married a handsome brave and borne him two children, both sons. Now, in her old age, she much enjoyed spending time with her granddaughters and their friends. They respected her years, as all Indian youths were taught to respect their elders, and they looked to her for guidance in womanly matters.

As her wrinkled fingers nimbly plucked the ripe red berries and deposited them in her basket, she kept a wary eye on the surrounding plain for enemies. One never knew when the Blackfeet might stage a raid, and there were always grizzlies to watch out for.

As alert as she was, she still didn't hear the rider approach, and had no idea they were no longer alone until she glanced up and saw the white man observing them. Although surprised that any white man could come up on them so quietly, she retained her composure. He was a big man on a fine black stallion, and nearby stood a great black dog. She stopped picking berries and greeted him in her tongue.

"Hello," the man said in the Crow language, and then he pointed at the village and used his hand in flawless sign language. "I seek Red Moon's people, Is that his village?"

"Yes," Stiff Back Woman responded. She saw no reason to lie to this man. He had an air of honorable character about him that impressed her. "But Red Moon is not there. He has not been seen in four or five moons."

"Is his grandson there?"

Stiff Back Woman frowned in sadness. "Little Sparrow died two moons ago. He was asking for his grandfather when he gave up the spirit."

The rider closed his eyes and seemed to tremble. When he opened his eyes again they were moist. "Thank you. Tell your people Red Moon is dead. Tell them he died bravely." With that the white man wheeled his horse and rode off, the dog keeping pace with the stallion.

"Wait!" Stiff Back Woman shouted, but it was no use. The rider went down the knoll and out across the prairie, and was soon lost in the dust raised by his mount.